The Mystery of the Nervous Lion

This Armada book belongs to:

_____

_____

_____

Alfred Hitchcock and
The Three Investigators

in

The Mystery of the
Nervous Lion

Text by Nick West

Based on characters created by Robert Arthur

Armada

First published in the U.K. in 1972 by
William Collins Sons & Co. Ltd., London and Glasgow.
First published in Armada in 1975 by
William Collins Sons & Co. Ltd., 14 St. James's Place,
London SW1A 1PF

Printed in Great Britain by
Love & Malcomson Ltd., Brighton Road,
Redhill, Surrey.

Contents

A Few Words from Alfred Hitchcock

GREETINGS and salutations! It is a pleasure to have you join me for another adventure with that remarkable trio of lads who call themselves The Three Investigators. This time a nervous lion leads them into a tangled web of mystery and excitement.

I imagine that you have already met The Three Investigators and know that they are Jupiter Jones, Bob Andrews, and Pete Crenshaw, all of Rocky Beach, California, a small community on the shores of the Pacific not far from Hollywood. But just in case this is your first meeting with the three, let me add that they make their Headquarters in a mobile home trailer cleverly hidden from sight in The Jones Salvage Yard. This fabulous junkyard is owned by Jupiter's aunt and uncle, for whom the trio works to earn spending money when they are not busy with their investigations.

Enough of introductions. On with the case! Our lion is growing nervous!

ALFRED HITCHCOCK

I

Empty Cages

JUPITER JONES turned his head at the sound of a horn and groaned. "Oh, no! Here comes my Uncle Titus with a lorryload for the yard. You know what that means—work!"

Pete Crenshaw and Bob Andrews followed Jupiter's despairing look. Coming through the big iron gates of The Jones Salvage Yard was a small lorry. Konrad, one of the two Bavarian yard helpers, was driving. Titus Jones, a small man with an enormous moustache, sat beside him.

As the lorry stopped, Mr Jones hopped off. Jupiter and his friends could see that the truck was filled with a lot of rusty pipes and other odds and ends. Some of the junk appeared to be broken cages.

Jupiter's Aunt Mathilda, who had been sitting in her wrought-iron garden chair outside the office cabin, leaped to her feet.

"Titus Jones!" she yelled. "Have you gone out of your senses? How do you expect to sell a lorryload of pipes and iron bars?"

"No problem, my dear," Titus Jones said, unruffled. He knew from past experience that

9

almost everything that interested him eventually sold to a buyer. And usually at a tidy profit. "Some of these bars come with cages."

"Cages?" his wife repeated. She came closer, squinting into the lorry. "You'd need some especially large canaries for those cages, Titus Jones."

"These are animal cages, woman," her husband declared. "Or rather, they used to be. I'll leave it to Jupiter and his friends here. Take a look, Jupiter. Could we put them to some use?"

Jupiter looked over the lot. "Well," he answered slowly, "they could be repaired, I suppose. New bars added, roofs put on, the cage floors mended, everything painted. We could do it, all right, but then what?"

"Then what?" his uncle roared. "Why then we'd have animal cages ready for them when they need them, wouldn't we?"

"When who needs them, Uncle Titus?" asked Jupiter.

"Why, the circus, my boy," his uncle replied. "Circus comes to town every year, don't it? Well, then, next time they come, we'll be ready in case they need some good solid cages for their brutes."

Jupe shrugged. "I guess so," he said doubtfully.

"You guess so!" his uncle roared. "Don't forget I spent my early years travelling with a circus. I guess I ought to know what they'd be looking for, wouldn't you say?"

Jupiter smiled. "Yes, Uncle Titus." He had

forgotten how proud his uncle was of his past association with the big top.

"Fine!" Titus said. "Hans! Konrad! Get this stuff off the lorry. Stack the cages separately so that we can get to work on them soon."

Konrad's brother, Hans, appeared from the back of the yard, and the Bavarian helpers began unloading the lorry. Uncle Titus got his pipe out, searched his pockets for a match, and slowly began puffing.

"Those cages," he began. "Got 'em for a song out in the valley. Found them with a lot of old junked cars. Feller didn't see much need for cages and such, so I bought the lot cheap. I'll be heading back in a while to try again. Just might be another load there."

He walked away puffing contentedly on his briar. Jupiter and his friends idly watched him go. Mrs Jones had a better idea of how the boys should pass their time.

"Jupiter!" she called. "Those iron bars and railings on the lorry should be stacked together. Perhaps we can sell them at a bargain price for the lot."

"Right, Aunt Mathilda," Jupe said. The stocky boy scrambled awkwardly up into the lorry with Pete and Bob. "Okay, fellows," he said. "You heard the order."

Pete Crenshaw stared down at the pile of rusty rails and bars. "It sure beats me, Jupe, where your uncle ever finds this junk. But what puzzles me even more is how he ever manages to sell it."

Jupiter grinned. "Uncle Titus has always been lucky that way, Pete. He's brought in stuff you'd swear nobody in the world would ever want, and sells it the very next day. So if he says he can sell these pipes, I believe it."

Bob put in, "Well, anyway, we get paid for working. And we can use the money. We need some new equipment for Headquarters."

Headquarters was a damaged mobile home trailer that Mr Jones had given to Jupiter to use as a meeting place for his friends. It was over at one side of the salvage yard, hidden by junk the boys had piled round it. Close by was Jupe's workshop section, fitted out with various tools and a printing press.

Inside Headquarters, the boys had equipped a tiny office with telephone, desk, tape recorder, and filing cabinets. There was also a small lab and a darkroom for developing pictures. Most of the equipment had been rebuilt by Jupe and his friends from junk that had come into The Jones Salvage Yard.

Bob, Pete, and Jupiter had started a puzzle-solving club originally, which they later turned into a junior detective firm called The Three Investigators. Although they had started the club in fun, they had solved several genuine mysteries that had come their way and had decided to pursue detective work more seriously.

Peter Crenshaw, the strongest member of the trio, now looked unhappily at the large pile of pipes remaining after the two big Bavarian helpers had unloaded the cages. "Okay," he said reluctantly, "might as well get started." He dragged out several long bars and hoisted them to his shoulder. "Where do you want them stacked, Jupe?" he asked, staggering under the heavy load.

Jupe pointed out an area near a shed. "We'll stack them in a pile there, Pete."

Pete grunted and backed off with his load. Jupe and Bob then took turns feeding the bars to Pete on return trips. Work progressed rapidly and soon the pile in the lorry was down to one.

Rubbing his hands, Pete stepped up. "All right, Jupe," he said, "I'll take that last little one now."

Jupe leaned forward to hand the bar over, and hesitated. He felt the weight of the bar again. "We'd better set this aside. It's just the size I've been looking for."

Bob looked puzzled. "For what? You starting your own junkyard now?"

"It just happens to be shorter than the rest," said Jupe. "We can use it for a slide bolt inside our headquarters door. For security reasons."

"Security?" Bob asked.

Jupe reddened. "I'm getting tired of crawling through our tunnel into Headquarters. There's got to be an easier way of doing things. I thought we might unlock the door."

Pete and Bob smiled at this roundabout explanation. The truth was that Jupiter was a little too fat to enjoy using their secret tunnel all the time.

Jumping off the lorry, Jupe walked over to Headquarters and the junk surrounding the trailer. "Maybe Uncle Titus won't need it," he said. "Or we can work off the price."

Pete wiped sweat from his brow. "I think we already did that. If you ask me, we did a good day's work in an hour."

"Okay, Jupe," Bob said. "Now what—?"

At that moment the red light mounted over their printing press blinked!

"A phone call!" Pete cried. "Maybe it's somebody wanting a mystery solved."

"I hope so," Jupe said excitedly. "We haven't had any to investigate in a long time."

Quickly they pushed aside the iron grillwork beside the printing press. Crawling through the box behind it, they entered Tunnel Two. This was a large corrugated pipe leading to a trap door in the floor of the hidden trailer. The boys rushed through on their hands and knees and surfaced in the small office of Headquarters.

Jupiter snatched up the ringing telephone.

"Jupiter Jones speaking," he said.

"One moment, please." A woman's voice could be heard clearly through the loudspeaker attachment Jupe had rigged up. "Mr Alfred Hitchcock is calling."

The three boys exchanged surprised and happy grins. As a rule, they found an exciting mystery waiting for them whenever Mr Hitchcock called.

"Hello there!" the famous director boomed. "Is this young Jupiter?"

"Yes, Mr Hitchcock," Jupe said.

"I hope you and your friends are not too busy just now. I have a friend who is in need of help, and I think you three lads are just the ones to solve his problem."

"We'd like to try, sir," Jupe said. "Can you give us an idea of your friend's problem?"

"Certainly," Mr Hitchcock said. "If you boys can arrange to be at my office tomorrow morning, I shall be happy to tell you all about it."

2

A Case in Lion Territory

SOME time ago, Jupiter and his friends had won the use of an antique Rolls-Royce, complete with chauffeur, in a contest. Their prize time eventually ran out, but then they helped a youthful client to gain an enormous inheritance. The grateful client arranged for the boys to have the use of the Rolls whenever needed. It had proved invaluable to them as investigators. Distances in southern California are vast, and it is difficult to cover them except by car.

Now Jupiter leaned forward and tapped the shoulder of the tall, English chauffeur, Worthington. "This will be fine, Worthington," he said. "Wait here. We won't be too long with Mr Hitchcock."

"Very good, Master Jones," Worthington replied. He guided the old, box-like automobile to a careful stop. Then he got out and held the door open for the boys. "I trust Mr Hitchcock has an interesting mission for you young gentlemen."

"We hope so, too, Worthington," Bob said. "Things have been kind of dull lately. We could use some excitement."

He quickly joined Jupe and Pete as they entered the Hollywood studio building where Mr Hitchcock had his office.

Alfred Hitchcock motioned them to seats in front of his big desk. He pushed some business correspondence aside and looked at the boys thoughtfully. Then casually he asked, "How comfortable are you lads with wild animals?"

Opposite him, The Three Investigators looked startled.

Jupiter cleared his throat. "It all depends on what kind of animals, sir, and the proximity involved. Given a reasonable distance between them and us and a measure of protection, I would say we are all quite at ease with them, and interested in their behaviour and habits."

"Jupe means we like them," Pete said. "It just goes against his nature to say something simple."

"Why, Mr Hitchcock?" asked Bob. "Is this about a mystery?"

"Perhaps," Mr Hitchcock said slowly. "And if not indeed a mystery, certainly a case that merits investigation. The wild animals I mentioned are part of the background where certain mysterious happenings are taking place."

Alfred Hitchcock paused. "Have you lads heard of a place called Jungle Land?"

"That's over in the valley near Chatwick," Bob replied. "It's some kind of wild-animal farm with lions and other animals roaming around. It's supposed to be a tourist attraction, I think."

"Yes," Alfred Hitchcock said. "The owner, Jim Hall, is an old friend. Lately he's run into a problem and I thought at once of you boys and your investigative talents."

"What's Mr Hall's problem exactly, sir?" asked Jupiter.

"It would appear he has a nervous lion," Mr Hitchcock said.

The boys looked at each other wide-eyed.

"To continue," Mr Hitchcock said. "Jungle Land is indeed open to the public. In addition, various movie companies at times rent the use of its premises. Its terrain and vegetation are suggestive of Western and African locales. Occasionally Jim Hall rents his animals. Some of them are wild, but several have been brought up gently and trained by Jim.

"Jim Hall's favourite lion is a remarkable example of his way with animals. This lion has been featured in many commercials for TV and has been used in films. It has always been a great attraction at Jungle Land and a good financial asset to Jim Hall."

"You mean, until now," Jupe said. "Your friend's lion is nervous and now he can't depend on it. That's his problem, isn't it?"

Alfred Hitchcock gave Jupiter a penetrating stare. "As usual, my astute young friend, your powers of deduction are equal to the task at hand. A film unit has rented the farm now to shoot sequences for a jungle film. Naturally Jim Hall cannot afford any accidents that might interfere with the film's speedy and successful completion. If anything were to go wrong, it would be ruinous to his entire operation."

"And we're supposed to go there and solve the mystery of the nervous lion," Jupe said. "Is that it?"

"Precisely," intoned Mr. Hitchcock. "Quickly and quietly. Without fuss or fanfare. And I need hardly add, without further disturbing the already unsettled lion."

Pete Crenshaw licked his lips. "How close do we have to get to this crazy cat?"

Alfred Hitchcock smiled affably. "Closeness is its own definition, young Peter. You will all be on the Jungle Land premises. Jim Hall's lion is there. And while ordinarily it might be considered reasonably safe to be in the lion's vicinity, I must warn you the situation has changed. A nervous lion—any nervous animal—can be dangerous."

The Three Investigators gulped.

"You can tell your friend Jim Hall not to

worry," said Bob. "His lion won't be the only nervous one there anymore."

"That's right," Pete added. "I'm not even there yet and I'm nervous already."

Mr Hitchcock turned to Jupiter. "Any further comment, young Jupiter, before I call my friend to say you lads are willing to undertake the assignment?"

Jupe shook his head. "No comment. But it might be a good idea to ask Mr Hall to put in a word for us with his lion!"

Mr Hitchcock smiled and picked up his phone. "I shall convey your message. And I shall expect a full report from you soon. Good-bye and good luck."

The Three Investigators waved and walked out wondering what kind of luck they could expect dealing with a nervous lion!

3

Welcome to Jungle Land

IT was past noon when The Three Investigators careered down the last steep grade of a narrow back road. Rolling mountains encircled the valley, which was a scant thirty minutes from Rocky

Beach. Jupiter's Uncle Titus had sent Konrad on a pickup job in nearby Chatwick and had allowed the boys to go along for their appointment in Jungle Land.

"Slow down, Konrad," Jupe ordered. "That's the place."

"Hokay, Jupe." The big Bavarian braked the small lorry to a jolting stop outside the main gate. The entrance sign read:

WELCOME TO JUNGLE LAND!
ADMISSION ONE DOLLAR, CHILDREN FIFTY CENTS

As the boys got out, they heard strange hooting and chattering cries. In the distance a loud trumpeting sound echoed in the hills. As if in answer to this challenge, there came a deep, rumbling roar that sent chills down their spines.

Konrad gestured to the gate. "You fellers going in there?" he asked. "You better watch it. I think I hear lions."

"There's nothing to worry about, Konrad," Bob said. "Mr Hitchcock wouldn't have sent us on this job if he thought it was really dangerous."

"We just have to look into something for the owner," Jupe said. "This is a safe tourist attraction."

Konrad shrugged. "Hokay," he said. "If you say it's safe, hokay. But better take care all the same. I be back for you a little later."

He waved and wheeled the lorry back to the main road. Soon the lorry was out of sight.

Jupe looked at his friends. "Well, what are we waiting for?"

Pete pointed to a small sign posted at the gate:

CLOSED TODAY

"I wondered why there wasn't anyone around," he said.

"It might be because the movie company is inside shooting," said Jupe.

Bob peered inside. "Shouldn't Mr Hall be here to meet us?"

Jupe nodded. "I expected him. But maybe he's busy with other things inside."

"Like his nervous lion," Pete said. "Maybe he's having a hard time convincing him we're not here for his dinner."

Jupe pressed on the gate. It opened to his touch.

"It's not locked," he said cheerfully. "That's either so the movie people can get in and out—or for us. Let's go."

The gate creaked shut behind them as they stepped inside. From beyond the trees, they heard chattering sounds punctuated by harsh screeches.

"Monkeys and birds," Jupe observed. "Harmless creatures."

"We'll find out soon enough," Bob said in a low voice.

The entrance road was narrow and twisting, bordered on either side by trees and thick foliage. Large curling vines looped down from trees.

"Looks like a jungle, all right," Pete observed.

The others nodded. As they advanced slowly, they cast suspicious glances at the dense under-growth on either side, wondering what strange creature might be crouching there waiting to spring. The odd sounds beyond continued, and again they heard the dull, reverberating roar.

They stopped at a signpost at a fork in the road.

"'Western Village and Ghost Town,'" Bob read on the sign pointing left. "What does the other say?"

Jupe was looking up at it quizzically. "To the animals," he said.

They turned right at the fork. After a few hundred yards, Pete pointed ahead. "There's a house. Maybe Mr Hall has his office there."

"It looks like a bunkhouse," Jupe said as they drew closer. "There's a corral behind it."

Suddenly there was a loud, ear-piercing scream. The boys froze, and then, as if with a single mind, dived into the shrubbery for cover.

Hidden behind the thick trunk of a barrel palm, Pete peered across the dirt road at the bunkhouse. Jupe and Bob, crouched behind a bush, also looked out anxiously. They waited for more sounds, their hearts beating fast. But now the thick jungle was silent.

"Jupe," Pete whispered. "What was that?"

Jupe shook his head. "I'm not sure. Maybe a cheetah."

"It could have been a monkey," Bob whispered.

They stayed in the shrubbery, waiting.

"Good grief!" Pete said hoarsely. "We came here

22

to find out about a nervous lion. Nobody said anything about nervous monkeys or cheetahs!"

"We've got to expect the animals here will be. making some kind of sounds," Jupe said. "It's only natural. Whatever that was, it's quiet now. Let's get to the house and find out what's happening."

The others hesitated as Jupe started forward, moving slowly and warily. Then they joined him.

"Anyway, that sound came from way up ahead," Pete muttered.

"Where the wild animals are locked up tight—I hope," Bob added.

"Come on," Jupe urged. "We're almost there."

The bunkhouse was old and needed paint. Pails and feedbins were scattered carelessly at the side. Tracks from many vehicles had carved deep ruts in the road. The corral fence sagged.

The old house stood silent, as if waiting for them.

"Now what?" Pete asked in a low voice.

Jupe stepped on to the low, slatted porch. There was a determined expression on his face. "We knock on the door," he said flatly, "and tell Mr Hall we're here."

He rapped vigorously. There was no response. "Mr Hall!" Jupiter called loudly.

Bob scratched his head. "Guess he's not home."

Pete held up his hand warningly. "Hold it!" he whispered. "I hear something."

They all heard it then. A low, muttering sound in an odd cadence. The sound came closer, approaching from the rear of the house. They could hear the crunching of footsteps on gravel. They drew back, eyes wide.

Suddenly it came at them, darting forward in an erratic line, head bobbing angrily. Yellow legs dug fiercely into the ground.

The Three Investigators stared.

4

Stalking a Lion

JUPITER JONES was the first to recover his voice. "Careful now!" he cautioned. "We don't want to be scared off by a mad rooster!"

"Gosh!" Pete said sheepishly. "Is that all it is?"

Bob let out a relieved sigh. "I never would have believed it!"

He looked down at the clucking black fowl that had sounded so ominous only a moment before, and laughed.

"Shoo, bird!" he yelled, waving his arms.

Startled, the cock lifted its black wings. Making angry sounds, it scuttled across the road, its high, red comb bobbing.

The boys all laughed.

"There's proof of how the mind can deceive

you," Jupe said. "We were intimidated by the jungle growth and the sounds of wild animals. We all expected something dangerous to be coming at us. We were conditioned for it."

He started for the door again.

"Hey, look over there, Jupe," Bob said.

The other boys followed Bob's pointing finger. In the shadows of the thick jungle, they caught a sudden movement. A figure in khaki stepped from behind a tree.

"Mr Hall!" Jupe yelled.

The man waited as the boys ran towards him.

"Hi," Pete said. "We've been looking for you."

The man looked at the boys questioningly. He was stocky and deep-chested, his faded safari shirt open at the throat. His light blue eyes contrasted vividly with the deep tan of his face. His nose was long and dented to one side. On his head was an old Aussie campaign hat, its wide brim folded over one ear.

As the boys came closer, he made an impatient movement with his hand. Something glinted.

Jupe and his friends stared down at the long, broad-bladed machete the man held carelessly at his side.

Jupiter spoke quickly. "We're The Three Investigators, Mr Hall. Didn't Mr Hitchcock tell you we were coming?"

The man blinked and looked surprised. "Oh, yes. Hitchcock. You say you're the three investigators?"

"That's right, Mr Hall," Jupe said. He reached

into his pocket and produced a business card on which was printed:

THE THREE INVESTIGATORS

"We Investigate Anything"

?   ?   ?

First Investigator – JUPITER JONES
Second Investigator – PETER CRENSHAW
Records and Research – BOB ANDREWS

"I'm Jupiter Jones. These are my partners, Pete Crenshaw and Bob Andrews."

"Nice to meet you, boys." He took the card and studied it. "What are the question marks for?"

"The question marks stand for things unknown," Jupiter explained. "For questions unanswered, riddles, enigmas. It's our business to answer those questions, unravel the riddles, and find solutions for the enigmas. That's why we're here. Mr Hitchcock told us about the trouble you're having with your nervous lion."

"Oh, he did?"

"Actually, he merely mentioned your lion was nervous. I imagine he expected you to fill in the details."

The stocky man nodded, and slipped the card into his shirt pocket. He frowned and squinted into the distance. There was a trumpeting sound, almost immediately followed by an answering roar.

"Well," he said smiling. "If you're feeling up to it, we can go out and have a look at him."

"That's what we're here for," said Jupe.

"Fine. Let's get moving then."

Turning abruptly, he skirted the bunkhouse and followed a faint trail through the jungle. The boys fell into step behind him.

"Perhaps you can fill us in on the way, Mr Hall," Jupe said, dodging a thick vine.

The long machete flashed in the air. The vine parted as if it were paper. "What d'ya want to know?" the man asked, resuming his rapid pace.

Jupe struggled to stay close behind. "Well, for example, all we know is that your lion is nervous. That's—well—rather unusual for a lion, isn't it?"

The man nodded, walking fast and slashing at the undergrowth looming in their path. "Not usual, at all. Know anything about lions?"

Jupiter gulped. "No, sir. That's why we'd like to know. It's curious, isn't it? I mean, this is a new development, isn't it?"

"Yep," the man said shortly. He held up his hand for silence. There were faint chattering sounds. Then came a booming roar. The man smiled. "Just up ahead," he said. "That's him out there." He cocked his head at Jupiter. "I'll leave it to you. Does he sound nervous?"

"I—I don't know. It sounds like—well, a normal lion roar." Jupe was determined to let Mr Hall know he wasn't the least bit nervous himself.

"That's right," the man said. He stopped for a moment, swishing his machete at the tall grass surrounding them. "Y'see, the lion is not a nervous animal, at all."

"But—" Jupe started, perplexed.

The man nodded. "Unless," he said, "unless somebody or something is making him that way. How does that strike you?"

The boys, together now, nodded.

"Sure, but what?" Bob asked.

The man shifted his position suddenly. "Don't move," he whispered. "Something out there."

Before they realised it, he had disappeared into the tall grass. They heard his footsteps, the swish of grass, and then suddenly nothing at all.

Somewhere overhead a bird screeched and they jumped nervously.

"Relax, fellows," Pete said. "That was only a bird."

"Only a bird!" Bob repeated. "Some bird! It sounded like a vulture."

The boys waited for several minutes. Jupe glanced at his watch. "I've a funny feeling that vulture is trying to tell us something," he said.

"Oh, come on, Jupe," Bob protested. "Tell us what?"

Jupe's face was pale. He licked his lips. "I have the feeling that Mr Hall isn't coming back. I think he's arranged some kind of test for us—to see how we react to the danger of the jungle."

"But why, Jupe?" asked Pete. "What would his

reason be? We're here to help him, aren't we? He knows that."

Jupe listened for a moment before answering. Strange calls came from high in the trees. Then once again they heard a deep, menacing roar.

Jupiter inclined his head in the direction of the last frightening sound. "I don't know what Mr Hall's reason can be. But I know that lion out there sounds a lot closer than before. He seems to be coming this way. I think that's what the vulture is telling us—that we're the prey! They usually circle a dead or soon-to-be-dead animal. In this case, us!"

Pete and Bob stared at Jupe. They knew he wasn't apt to joke in serious circumstances. Instinctively the three boys moved closer together.

They listened tensely.

They heard the swish of grass. Then footfalls, soft and stealthy.

Holding their breath, they edged closer to a large tree.

Then, almost directly behind them, they heard a blood-chilling sound—*the roar of the lion!*

5

Dangerous Game

"QUICK!" Jupe whispered urgently. "Up this tree! It's our only chance!"

In an instant the three had scrambled up a smoothboled gum tree. They huddled breathlessly in its fork barely ten feet from the ground, looking intently at the waist-high grass beyond.

Pete pointed towards a thick cluster of growth. "I—I just saw some grass bend there. You hear it? Something is moving—"

He blinked at a soft call, a whistle from the high grass. Then to the amazement of all three, a young boy stepped out of the brush, peering cautiously about.

"Hey!" Bob called. "Up here!"

The boy whirled. In the same motion, he swung a rifle upward. "Who are you?" he demanded.

"F-friends," Bob gasped weakly. "Put down that gun."

"We've been invited here," Pete added. "We're The Three Investigators."

"We're waiting for Mr Hall to come back," Jupe put in. "He left us waiting while he went out there to investigate something."

The boy swung the rifle down. "Come down out of there," he said.

Cautiously the three slid down the trunk. Jupe pointed into the grass. "We heard a lion out there a little while ago. We thought we'd be safer up in the tree."

The boy smiled. He appeared to be about their age. "That was George," he said.

Pete gulped. "George? The lion's name is George?"

The boy nodded. "You don't have to be afraid of George. He's friendly."

A deep roar came from the high grass. It sounded terrifyingly close.

The Three Investigators stiffened.

"Y-you call that roar friendly?" Pete asked.

"I suppose you've got to get used to it first. But that's George—and he wouldn't harm anybody."

A twig snapped sharply. Bob paled. "What makes you so sure?"

"I work here," he boy answered, smiling. "I see George every day. By the way, my name's Mike Hall."

"We're glad to meet you, Mike," said Jupe. He introduced himself and his companions. Then, "I'm not sure we appreciate your father's sense of humour."

Mike Hall looked surprised.

"Bringing us out here and then deserting us with a lion close by," Pete burst in heatedly. "That's no joke."

"That's probably why he's in trouble here,"

Bob added. "You can lose a lot of people trying to help you if you play games like that."

The youth looked at the three angry investigators, puzzled. "I don't understand. First, I'm Jim Hall's nephew, not his son. Second, Jim wouldn't have left you here with the lion. We've all been looking for him—George got out somehow, and we forgot you were coming, in the excitement. I've heard George roaring and been trying to catch up with him."

Jupe listened to this explanation calmly. "I'm sorry, Mike. We're telling the truth. Mr Hall led us out here and then abandoned us. The lion roared out there, and he told us to wait. He disappeared into the grass—and—well, we've had a long wait—and a worried one!"

Mike shook his head stubbornly. "There must be some mistake. That couldn't have been Jim. I've been with him all day and I just left him. You must have met somebody else. What did he look like?"

Bob described the stocky man with the Aussie campaign hat. "We called him Mr Hall and he didn't deny it," he added.

"He carried a long machete," Pete said, "and knew how to use it. He also knew his way around. He cut his way right to this spot to show us the lion."

Jupe added, "I suppose we can't blame you for sticking up for your uncle, Mike, but—"

"I'm not," Mike interrupted angrily. "That man you described was Hank Morton. He used to work here as an animal trainer and handler."

He stared out at the high grass, listening intently. "What I don't understand is how he got here. My Uncle Jim fired him."

"Fired him?" Jupe asked. "What for?"

"He was cruel to the animals, for one thing," Mike said. "My Uncle Jim won't stand for that. For another, he's mean—a troublemaker. He drinks a lot. When he's in that condition, he doesn't know what he's doing."

"Perhaps," Jupe said thoughtfully. "But if that was Hank Morton who brought us out here, he wasn't the least bit drunk. He was cold sober—and knew exactly what he was doing."

"But why?" Bob asked. "Why did he do it? What was his idea—marooning us out here?"

"I don't know," Mike Hall said. "Perhaps—" His eyes gleamed. "Did you tell him anything—about why you're here?"

Jupe clapped his head ruefully. "That's it! We told him Alfred Hitchcock sent us to see him about his nervous lion. I recall now that he looked surprised at first."

"I can think of a reason," Pete said. "He was trying to get even with Jim Hall for firing him. We just happened along conveniently."

"But why us?" asked Bob. "We've got nothing to do with Jim Hall and his getting fired."

"The nervous lion," Jupe reminded. "The case we're on and the reason we're here. Perhaps he didn't want us to find out why that lion is nervous."

"That could be it," young Mike Hall said. "And Hank Morton probably let George get loose, too. George couldn't have got out by himself."

"Well," said Jupe. "When we see your uncle, he might have a better explanation. I suggest we start back now, Mike, and have a talk with him."

"I don't think we can do that right now," Bob said quietly.

Jupe looked at Bob, surprised. "Why not?" What's wrong with that idea?"

Bob's voice was low and shaking. "It's—right behind you, fellows. A great big lion just came out of the brush. Maybe it's George—but he sure doesn't look friendly!"

Mike turned around. "It's George, all right. But he knows me. Just don't make any sudden movements, fellows. I'll handle him."

The boys watched uneasily as Mike took a step forward. He lifted one hand, carefully extending it palm up. "All right, George. Easy now, fellow. Nice boy, George."

His reassuring voice was answered by a snarl. Slowly and menacingly a massive, thick-maned lion advanced. Its head was down and its huge yellow eyes were narrowed. It turned its big head to one side and snarled again. Less than ten feet away it halted. The huge jaws opened, exposing long, frightening fangs.

Then, with a deep roar rumbling in its throat, the lion came forward again.

The Three Investigators stared at it helplessly, unable to move, their throats tight with fear.

Mike was speaking again. "Easy, George," he said quietly. "Easy, boy. You know me, fellow. Easy now. Nice and easy."

The huge, tawny beast flicked its tail. A low rumble came rolling like thunder. It came forward another step.

Young Mike shook his head. "Something's wrong, fellows. George knows me. But he isn't acting his usual friendly way."

Slowly, the boy backed away.

The lion came on.

6

A Narrow Escape

THE Three Investigators stood rooted to the ground as inch by inch young Mike Hall retreated before the advancing lion. His voice was still low and friendly but the lion ignored it.

Jupiter Jones was as paralysed with fear as his companions. But his brain was still active. He was puzzled by the lion's behaviour towards somebody it knew. It gave no sign that it recognised young Mike Hall.

Suddenly Jupe discovered what was wrong. He tried to keep his voice low and not attract the lion's attention.

"Look at his left foreleg, Mike," he said. "He's wounded!"

Mike looked quickly at the lion's leg. It was covered by a thick film of blood.

"No wonder George isn't obeying," said Mike softly. "I'm afraid I've got bad news for you guys. A hurt animal is dangerous. I don't know if I can handle him."

"You've got a rifle," Bob whispered. "Maybe you ought to shoot."

"This is only a .22 calibre. It wouldn't do more than tickle George. It might make him even madder. I just carry it for emergencies, for firing a warning shot."

The lion took another step forward. The huge beast winced as the bloody leg took its weight. Its mouth opened in a twisting snarl.

The Three Investigators inched backward to the gum tree. Mike saw their movement and shook his head.

"Don't try it, fellows," he cautioned. "He'd be on you before you got one leg up."

"Okay, Mike," said Jupe. "But why not fire a warning shot? Wouldn't that scare George off?"

Mike smiled grimly. "Not a chance. He's got his head down. That means his mind is made up and nothing is going to change it." He bit his lip. "I just wish my Uncle Jim was here."

A soft whistle trilled from the high grass. Abruptly a tall, bronzed man stepped out.

"You've got your wish, Mike," he said dryly.

"Now nobody moves, nobody talks except me, understand?"

The man stepped lithely forward. "Now, Georgie, what's going on here?" he asked pleasantly.

The words were spoken in a light, conversational tone. They had their effect. The lion turned its head towards the man. Its long tail flicked. Then, cocking its head, it opened its jaws and roared.

The tall man nodded. "I see," he said softly. "You're hurt. Is that it?"

Then to the amazement of the boys, he strode up to the lion and took its huge head in his hands.

"Come on, George," he said. "Let's have a look at it."

The lion opened its jaws again. The expected roar became a moaning sound instead. Slowly it extended its bleeding leg.

"Oh, it's your leg, is it?" asked Jim Hall. "Okay, old fellow, take it easy. I'll take care of it for you."

He removed a handkerchief from his pocket and bent to one knee. Deftly, he bandaged the wound, his face dangerously close to the lion's jaws.

The lion stood patiently as Jim Hall knotted the handkerchief. The man rose. He rubbed the lion's ears and twisted his mane. Then, affectionately, he pounded the beast's shoulders.

"There you are, George—almost as good as new."

Smiling, he turned away. The lion's voice rumbled in its thick throat. Its muscles quivered.

Then suddenly there was a quick, blurring yellow movement. Instantly Jim Hall was down, the lion upon him.

"Look out!" Pete cried.

The Three Investigators looked on in horror as the man writhed under the weight of the big jungle cat.

Jupe turned to Mike Hall. The boy was watching calmly, a slight smile on his lips. Jupe couldn't understand. "Do something!" he shouted.

"Use your gun, Mike!" Bob yelled.

Mike Hall lifted his hand. "It's nothing to worry about, fellows. They're only playing. George was brought up by Jim and loves him."

"But—" Jupe started to say. His eyes bugged out as he saw the huge lion thrown aside by Jim Hall. With a ferocious snarling sound, it lashed back, wrapping its forelegs around the man's shoulders. It opened its jaws wide, its large teeth inches from the man's face.

Unbelievably, Jim Hall laughed!

He braced to confront the snarling lion, and as he was knocked aside, pounded its ribs and yanked at the long mane. The animal moaned and flicked its long tail. Then to the utter bewilderment of the boys, it rolled over on its back, a strange sound coming from its throat.

"He's purring!" Bob exclaimed.

Jim Hall sat up and dusted himself off. "Whew!" he said in mock dismay. "That cat's a lot heavier than he thinks! It was easier when George was a cub."

Jupiter sighed his relief. He turned to Mike. "That just about scared me out of my wits. Do they always play that rough?"

"It scared me too when I first saw them at it," Mike admitted. "But I'm used to it now. George is so well-trained, he acts like a big overgrown puppy. You can see how good-natured he really is, now."

Jupe narrowed his eyes. "But Mr Hitchcock said—" He turned to the tall man stroking the lion's chest. "Mr Hall, we're The Three Investigators. Alfred Hitchcock told us you were having trouble, that your lion was nervous for some reason."

"That's right, son," Jim Hall said. "Take what happened here. Ol' George never acted that way before. He knows Mike and never should have come on that mean and ornery. I've brought him up, so naturally he listens to me, but lately he hasn't been dependable, at all."

"Maybe we can find out why," Jupe offered. "That wound on his leg, for example. Does that strike you as an accident?"

"What do you mean?"

"It looked like a slashing cut," Jupe said. "Something that could have been made by a long, sharp instrument—a machete, for instance."

The man nodded. "Yes. But—"

"When we arrived, we mistook another man for you, sir. He led us out here and he was wielding a machete—"

"It was Hank Morton," Mike interrupted. "Jupe

39

described him to me. He must have let George loose."

Jim Hall's jaw set grimly. "Hank Morton was here? When I fired him, I warned him not to come back." He looked at his lion, puzzled. "*Somebody* let George out. It might have been Hank. You say he brought you out here?"

"Yes," Bob put in. "Then he left us and went off into the high grass, telling us to wait."

"If he used to handle your lion, maybe he was able to get close enough to wound him with that machete, and make him mad enough to go for *us*," Pete said.

"If he did," Jim Hall said angrily, "that will be Hank Morton's last trick. Because if I don't catch up with him for that, *George will!*"

He tugged at the lion's ears affectionately. "Come on, boy. We're going to have Doc Dawson take a look at you."

Mike answered Jupe's inquiring look. "Doc Dawson is our veterinarian. An animal doctor. He takes care of George and all our other animals here."

Jim Hall led his lion off through the jungle. "Come along, boys. I'll fill you in on what's been happening when we get back to the house. Alfred Hitchcock said you fellows were pretty good at unravelling mysteries. Maybe you can spot what's wrong. Because sure as shooting, something is going on around here that I can't figure out."

7

The Trouble with George

"HERE we are."

Jim Hall stopped at a small covered van parked on a side road. He dropped the tail-board, urged George up, then fastened it in place.

"Come on," Mike said to Jupe and his friends. "We'll sit up front with Jim."

The Jungle Land owner got behind the wheel and started the vehicle. As he backed and turned the van round, Jupe leaned forward.

"How did George get out, Mr Hall? Where do you usually keep him—in his own compound?"

Jim Hall shook his head. "He stays in our house —with Mike and me. I don't know how he got out unless Hank Morton saw me leave. He could have let him out then. George was used to him being around so that would have been no problem. Once George was out, he could have wandered anywhere. That's what had me worried," he added, his lips tightening.

He followed the narrow, winding road up a hill and swung up a gravel drive leading to a large white house.

"Here we are," he announced. "Run inside and call Doc Dawson, will you, Mike?"

As Mike jumped off, Jupiter looked around in surprise. "Is this where you live? We thought that first one we came to—the bunkhouse—"

"That's for show," Jim Hall answered, smiling. "People come to Jungle Land for a lot of reasons. It's an animal farm and ranch, and we throw in a bit of the old Wild West for them, too. Sometimes we use the place for filming movies. One is being shot right now, matter of fact—a jungle picture."

"So Mr Hitchcock told us," Jupe said. "He led us to believe that was your concern at the moment, your lion not being trustworthy while a movie was being made here."

"Correct," Hall said. "George happens to be rented out, too, for the production. If he forgets he's supposed to be gentle and doesn't respond to my commands, Jay Eastland might lose a valuable leading man."

"Who's Jay Eastland?" Bob asked.

"That name sounds familiar," Pete said. "My dad does special effects for film companies. I'm sure I've heard him mention Jay Eastland's name."

Jim Hall said, "Eastland is a very important film producer and director—at least, he thinks he is."

He turned to unfasten the tail-board of the van. Mike Hall, who had just come out of the house, whistled and pointed to an approaching cloud of dust.

"Here comes trouble, Uncle Jim," he called.

Jim Hall looked up, his brow darkening.

"Trouble is right—here it comes in the person of Mr Eastland himself."

The cloud of dust cleared to reveal a station wagon. In a few seconds it pulled up and stopped. A short, beefy, bald-headed man hopped out of the back seat. He advanced with jerky steps, his face flushed and angry.

"Hall," he shouted, "I'm holding you to the terms of our contract."

Jim Hall looked down at the perspiring director. "I don't know what you're talking about, Eastland. "What's up?"

Eastland shook his fist at the animal owner. "That contract states no danger to myself or my people, remember? I guess you have a good explanation for what's happened?"

Jim Hall's eyebrows flew up. "My contract and agreement stand," he said coldly. "What happened?"

"Rock Randall's been hurt," Eastland yelled. "One of your animals got loose and attacked him —that's what happened!"

"That's impossible!" Hall said firmly.

The angry visitor pointed accusingly at the big lion in the rear of the van.

"There's all the proof I need, right there! Your pet lion! I happen to know he was loose and roaming around an hour ago. I'd like to hear you deny it!"

"You're right, Eastland. George was loose for a time. But that's no proof he attacked Randall. I can't believe it."

"You'll believe it when you see him," Eastland sneered.

"Is he hurt badly?" asked Hall quickly.

Eastland shrugged. "Let's say that being attacked by a bad-tempered lion doesn't do anybody any good."

Jim Hall's lips tightened. "Now, hold on there. We still don't know for certain George did it."

"Who else could do a job like that? Wait till you see—"

"I'm going to do that right now," Jim Hall snapped. "Just as soon as I lock George in the house."

As he lowered the tail-board, a horn sounded. A small old lorry came bouncing around the turn.

"It's Doc Dawson," Mike Hall whispered to the boys.

The driver braked to a skidding halt and jumped out. He was tall and thin. Under his grizzled moustache jutted the stub of an unlit cigar. He hurried towards the group with long strides, carrying a black leather medical bag.

The visitor stopped as he saw the lion in the van. Ignoring Eastland, he addressed Jim Hall in a gruff voice. "Got here as fast as I could, Jim, after Mike's call. What's that about George being hurt?"

"Flesh wound on his leg, Doc," Jim answered. "Somebody let George out while Mike and I were away. We rounded him up north of the bunkhouse."

"It looks like somebody cut him with a knife or machete, Doc," Mike Hall put in.

The angular vet turned to Mike, frowning. "Who could have done that to old George? I'd better have a look. Hold him steady for me, will you, Jim?"

The vet leaned forward as Jim Hall held the lion's mane. "Let's have a look, Georgie, boy," the vet said softly.

He slipped off the handkerchief bandage and lifted the lion's leg. The animal whimpered.

"Come on, George," the vet said. "I won't hurt you. Been taking care of you since you were a baby."

After a cursory glance, Dawson dropped the leg. "Superficial cut, Jim, but nasty. I'd better take him back to the dispensary for a better look. We don't want to risk an infection."

"Right," Jim Hall said. "You're going with Doc Dawson, George," he informed the lion, guiding him down the slanted tail-board.

As the vet started for his truck, the irate film producer stepped in his way. "What's going on?" he bellowed. "Where you taking that lion? We hired him for the movie. He starts work tomorrow morning at eight sharp."

Doc Dawson stopped to light his stub of cigar and blew smoke in Eastland's face. "That lion will be ready to work when I say he is. His leg may be better by tomorrow morning, and then again it may not. My job is to keep George healthy. I don't care two cents for your crummy movie. Now get out of my way, mister, or I'll walk right over you!"

Jupe and his companions quietly watched the drama. At the sudden vehemence in the vet's voice, Eastland paled and backed off. Dawson opened the rear door of his truck. Jim Hall brought George forward, patted the lion's flank, and raised his hand.

"Up you go, Georgie."

Obediently, the lion leaped into the truck. Hall closed the door and Dawson drove off. The lion pressed against the open-mesh sides of the truck, looking sad, a whimpering sound in its throat.

Eastland stepped forward again. "I'm telling you now, Hall, that lion better be ready," he threatened. "Now do you want to see what he did to Rock Randall, or not?"

Without a word, Jim Hall followed the film producer into his station wagon. He waved to Mike as the driver spun the long car around, calling as he caught Jupe's eye, "Sorry, fellows— I'll see you later."

Jupe watched thoughtfully until the station wagon disappeared into the jungle. "That sounds like a bad scene, if it's true," he said.

"If what's true?" Mike Hall snapped. "My Uncle Jim's story or Mr Eastland's?"

Jupe shrugged. "I'm not disputing your uncle's word, Mike. But you have to admit he looked worried."

"I'm sorry, Jupe," Mike said, his voice breaking. "I didn't mean to flare up at you. But anything that concerns my uncle, concerns me, too. I—well, I'm living with him because my parents were killed in a car accident. He's my father's brother, and my only family now—except for Cal."

"Cal?" asked Bob.

"Who's he?" Pete put in.

"Cal Hall is my other uncle. He's a big game hunter and explorer in Africa," Mike explained. "He sends Jim animals for Jungle Land. If Jim gets them young enough, like with George, he can train them easily. He puts the others on exhibit here and hopes to train them all some day. But it's a lot harder to do once they're full grown."

"How come Jay Eastland acts so nasty?" Pete asked. "What's he got against your Uncle Jim?"

"Nothing I know of," Mike said. "He's worried about his movie getting done on schedule. And before he leased Jungle Land, he wanted an agreement it would be safe working here, with the animals around. Jim guaranteed it would."

"What happens if your uncle guessed wrong—and there's an accident?" Bob asked.

"Jim would lose a lot of money. He had to put up a bond of fifty thousand dollars as a guarantee. He signed over Jungle Land as security for the bond. So he could lose everything. He's losing money already because tourists aren't allowed in when we rent out for a movie. They might disrupt things."

Jupiter listened carefully. "I assume, though, that your uncle will make a considerable amount of money if the movie goes through on schedule, without any accidents. Correct?"

"Yes," Mike admitted. "I don't know the exact

amount but it's so much a day. And George gets paid five hundred dollars when he works. Trained animals are rented for a lot of money—just like movie stars."

"Has George had any accidents before?" asked Jupe. "Has he ever attacked anybody?"

"No," Mike said. "Never. He's a very gentle animal and well-trained. That is—" he bit his lip "—until lately, anyway. Recently he's been acting up."

Bob, in charge of Records and Research, had his little memo book open. "We still have no information about that," he said. "How has George been acting? What's he doing now that he didn't do before? Maybe that might give us a hint, Mike, about what's making him nervous."

"Well, he's not himself. He's on edge. He stays in the house with us but lately he hasn't slept well. Almost every night, he's up and growling, walking around, trying to get out. Jim can't get him to go back to sleep, and he doesn't take orders as he used to. He's getting so hard to handle now I'm afraid he's not the good-natured, well-trained animal he used to be."

"It could be something outside is exciting him," Jupe said. "Are any animals here allowed to roam loose at night?"

Mike shook his head. "We have deer in a compound but they can't get out. We have horses that are used in a lot of Westerns. They're kept in a corral. We've got two elephants down by the lake but they're in their own compound, too, and stay there. We've got raccoons, monkeys, birds, dogs, chickens, and a lot of other animals—but they're all penned up at night and accounted for."

"Nevertheless," Jupe said, "something or somebody is making George nervous."

"Nervous enough, maybe, to attack that actor, Rock Randall," said Pete. "Though maybe he asked for it. I remember hearing he's a pretty nasty guy."

"He'd have to be pretty stupid as well as nasty to start up with George," Bob said. "George didn't look too friendly and gentle when we ran into him. Maybe it was because he got that cut on his leg. Maybe not."

"We can't say anything for sure yet, fellows," Jupe said. "We can't blame George for Randall's accident until Jim comes back and tells us what happened. Maybe it was another kind of accident. One that none of the animals here were—"

Mike clapped his hands suddenly. "The gorilla!" he cried.

"What gorilla?" Pete asked.

"Do you have a gorilla here, too?" Bob said.

"Not yet—but we're expecting one. Part of a new shipment from my Uncle Cal. Maybe it got here already, and got loose—and attacked Rock Randall!"

Jupe held his hand up. "Assuming it already got here how could it escape? Wouldn't it be in a locked cage?"

Mike nodded. "You're right. I'm acting as nervous as George, myself. Jim didn't say anything about the gorilla arriving, and he'd know. Besides, if it was here, there's no way it could get out of its cage unless—unless—"

"Unless what, Mike?" asked Bob.

The young boy licked his lips. "Unless somebody who didn't like my Uncle Jim opened its cage and let it out!"

8

A Tough Customer

IT was still early afternoon and The Three Investigators were on their way back to The Jones Salvage Yard with Konrad. Their time had run out before Jim Hall returned. The boys left Mike with the promise that they would return at the earliest opportunity.

Konrad, already waiting for them outside the Jungle Land gate, looked relieved when they came out. "You look hokay," he said. "I guess maybe you get along all right with that lion inside."

"He sounds a lot tougher than he is, Konrad," Jupe said. "We'll see what happens next time."

The big Bavarian shook his head dubiously. "You coming back here again? You push your luck too much maybe, Jupe."

Jupe smiled. "I don't think so, Konrad. At least, I hope not. Anyway, we're involved in a mystery and we'll have to keep coming back until it's solved."

Konrad only shook his head again and started the lorry, remaining gloomily silent on the trip home.

The boys resumed their conversation.

"We have one possible suspect anyway," Bob said. "Hank Morton. He has a motive for letting George out—to get even for being fired. I'd suspect Jay Eastland, too, but what could his motive be? I don't see that he gains anything by delaying his movie. Usually they try to get them done on time, don't they, Pete?"

"Sure," Pete replied. "I've heard it from my dad often. Film companies have a limited budget and a tight schedule, as a rule. Especially so when they're working on location, like Mr Eastland is now at Jungle Land. What do you think, Jupe?"

"I'm not certain yet what to think," their stocky leader said slowly. "It could be an act of revenge on Hank Morton's part. Or something to do with Jim Hall's putting up his whole operation as security for his animals' good behaviour while the movie is being shot. He stands to lose an awful lot if anything goes wrong. Too much, if you ask me."

"Anyway, that's not what we came out for," Pete said. "It was because of a nervous lion, remember? Nothing anybody's said so far deals with that. We still don't know what's making George nervous."

"That's true," Jupe admitted. "And for all we know, the lion getting out of the house and then being wounded could have been purely accidental. He could have jumped out of a window, or the wind might have blown a door open. He could have cut his leg any number of ways. His nervousness is something else."

"Maybe what they need there is a good animal psychologist instead of a vet," said Bob.

Konrad interrupted their speculations by announcing their arrival at the salvage yard with a warning blast of his horn.

Jupe looked up surprised. "Thanks, Konrad. You made good time."

"I go back that way again for more pickup stuff tomorrow," Konrad said. "In case you fellows still got business with that lion."

"Swell, Konrad," said Jupe. "I'll let you know if we're going."

The boys jumped out of the cab as Konrad continued to the far end of the junkyard. Jupe started towards Headquarters, then stopped abruptly, an astonished look on his face.

"They're gone!" he cried.

"What's gone?" Pete asked.

"The bars!" Jupe exclaimed. "That whole stack we unloaded from the lorry yesterday morning. All gone! Uncle Titus must have made a fast deal."

Bob scratched his head, puzzled. "Who would

want to buy a lorryload of rusty iron bars?"

Jupe shrugged. "I don't know. But it's the kind of luck my uncle always has."

Bob looked over Jupe's shoulder and groaned. "Uh-oh! Here comes your aunt, Jupe. She's got that look in her eye that means work!"

Jupiter turned to face his aunt. "Were you looking for us, Aunt Mathilda?"

"Indeed I was," his aunt said. "Where were you boys? A customer came and bought up all those iron bars, and there wasn't a soul around to help him load them."

Jupiter explained that Uncle Titus had given them permission to ride with Konrad on his trip to Chatwick. "Wasn't Hans around?" he asked.

"Indeed he wasn't," his aunt replied. "He was off again with your uncle to pick up some more of those bars. Apparently he's found a place that has plenty of them cheap."

Jupe smiled. "All right, Aunt Mathilda. We'll try to be around if that customer returns for more of the same."

"I wouldn't be at all surprised if he did," his aunt said. "So mind you are here tomorrow." As she turned to go, she added over her shoulder, "And by the way, I've fixed up a stack of sandwiches. They're in the office. You and your friends might be hungry."

As the boys started happily off towards the office cabin, Mathilda Jones added, "And when you've finished, Jupiter, you'll have to mind the office. I have to go downtown to do some shopping now. Titus should be back soon."

"All right, Aunt Mathilda," Jupe said.

"Konrad is driving me in the small lorry," Mrs Jones said. "Now mind you don't leave, and don't miss any sales, Jupiter."

"I won't. Don't worry."

Mrs Jones nodded and walked away.

Inside the small office, the boys found piles of sandwiches wrapped in wax paper and several bottles of root beer and orange pop.

"Too bad, Jupe, about having to work tomorrow," Pete said, wolfing down a thick sandwich. "I was ready to go back to Jungle Land and have Mike show us around."

"We'd have some news then," Bob said, "about what happened to Rock Randall. If George really did it, they're in big trouble."

Jupe looked glum. "We still have a lot of work ahead of us at Jungle Land. We don't know the terrain at all yet. And there are far too many possibilities of what might be going on at night. Mike stated that George became nervous and restless at that time. So we'll have to check that out." He scowled. "Animals tend to become restless before an approaching storm. But Mike didn't mention the weather. Far as I can recall, it's been pretty good the past month. If not that, then who or what could be making the lion nervous? It's still a complete mystery."

"Why did Hank Morton pretend to be Jim Hall and bring us out to where George was?" asked

54

Bob. "If you ask me, that's a mystery, too. What did he have against us?"

"I don't know," answered Jupe. "But notice another curious thing. George was roaring before we got to him. It's possible that Hank Morton did not inflict that wound. No," he concluded, shaking his head, "I'm afraid next time we go back we'll have to keep our eyes and ears open. We have to learn a lot more than we know."

Pete noticed a movement out the window. "Uh-oh, Jupe—I think you have a customer. Somebody just came in. Didn't your aunt tell you not to miss any sales?"

A dark saloon had pulled into the salvage yard. A light-haired man was looking around the neatly arranged junk. He walked quickly around the piles, lifting objects off the top to peer behind and below. Seeming unsatisfied, he wiped dust from his hands and turned to the door of the office.

Jupe was standing there waiting. Bob and Pete were behind him, ready to help.

The customer was thin and broad-shouldered, wearing a business suit and a bow tie. His eyes were very pale blue and his face had a curious, hatchet-like shape, wide at the cheekbones and tapering abruptly to a narrow, pointed chin. When he spoke, his voice had the toughness of a man used to giving orders.

"I'm looking for some iron bars," he said. He looked at Jupe questioningly. "Is the owner around?"

"No, sir," Jupe replied. "But I work here. I'm

55

sorry, but we don't have any more iron bars. We just sold the whole stack of them."

"What? When was this—who bought them?"

"Earlier today, I guess. I don't know who purchased them, sir."

"Why not?" the man demanded. "Don't you people keep records of your sales here?"

"Only of money received," Jupiter said. "Whoever bought those iron bars loaded and transported them himself. So we have no record of delivery. In a junkyard business like this, people generally just come in, pick what they want, and take it home with them."

"I see," the man said. He looked around again, disappointed.

"My Uncle Titus, the owner, is out now," Jupe said. "He might be hauling back some more iron bars. If you care to leave your name and address, he could get in touch with you."

"That's a thought," the man said. His eyes kept darting about the junk piled in the yard. "But so far as you know, there's not a single bar available now, big or small. Is that right?"

"Yes, sir," Jupe said. "I'm sorry. Maybe if you told me what you wanted them for, I might be able to find something else here you could use as a substitute."

The man shook his head. "I'm not interested in any substitutes." He suddenly pointed, his voice loud and triumphant. "What's that over there? What are you trying to do, kid—hold out on me?"

Jupe looked in the direction in which the man

56

was pointing. "Those are animal cages," he said.

"I know they are," the man said nastily. "But they have bars, don't they?"

Jupe shrugged. "Some do and some don't. We have to repair those cages, replace the missing bars, rebuild and repaint the tops and bottoms, you see, and—"

"Never mind all that," the man said impatiently. "I'm just interested in buying the iron bars. As many as I can get. How much?"

He took a thick wallet out and started to leaf through a number of notes.

Jupiter blinked. "You want the bars? Not the cages?"

"That's right, genius. How much?"

Jupe frowned. He remembered his uncle's plans to fix up the cages for the circus. Jupiter never questioned what his uncle wanted, nor his reasons.

"I'm sorry," he said. "Those bars aren't for sale. We need them to complete the cages so they can be sold to the circus."

The man grinned. "Okay," he said. "That's fine. That's just what I want—circus cages. I'll take them as is, and fix them up myself. How much?"

Again he riffled the thick pile of notes impatiently.

"Do you work for a circus?" Jupe asked.

"What's the difference?" the man snapped. "I want circus cages, and you got them. How much kid? C'mon. I'm in a hurry."

Jupe looked speculatively at the cages. There were four of them, all in extremely poor condition.

"That would be one thousand dollars," he said sleepily.

The man's fingers tightened on his wallet. "A thousand dollars for that junk? Are you kidding? Take a look at them—they're falling apart!"

Jupe heard Bob and Pete clear their throats nervously behind him. He looked again at the cages, then very deliberately at the man. "That would be one thousand dollars apiece," he said distinctly. "Four thousand dollars for all four."

The hatchet-faced man stared at Jupiter and slowly replaced his wallet in his pocket. "Maybe you shouldn't be left alone to run a business, kid. I can get new cages for that kind of money."

Jupe shrugged. Having been a child actor when he was very young, he appreciated the scene he was playing now. "Perhaps you can, sir. I've no idea what the current market price is for new circus cages. If you should care to drop back when my uncle is here, perhaps he might give you a more satisfactory price."

The visitor shook his head impatiently. "I don't have time for that, kid." He brought a note out of his pocket and offered it. "Here's twenty dollars for the lot. Take it or leave it. My guess is your uncle bought the whole lot for five dollars. That's all junk, kid." He waved the twenty-dollar note under Jupe's nose. "Well, what do you say? Twenty dollars?"

Jupiter sucked in his breath, hesitating. He knew the man was right. The bars as well as the cages were practically worthless. But he had learned to trust his instincts.

"Sorry," he said, turning away. "No deal."

He saw the man's hand dart to his pocket. For a long moment, Jupe held his breath, wondering if he had made a mistake.

9

More Trouble

THE hatchet-faced man's voice was cold and threatening. "All right, kid—have it your way. I'll be back!"

The man quickly got into his car, started his engine, and roared out of the salvage yard.

Jupe slumped, blowing out his cheeks in a long, relieved sigh.

"Good grief!" Bob exclaimed. "What was that all about?"

"A thousand dollars for each of those crummy cages?" Pete asked sarcastically. "I bet that man was right—that your uncle didn't pay more than five dollars for the lot—including the loose bars and pipes that we stacked."

Jupe nodded, feeling deflated. "I know," he said. "Uncle Titus hardly ever pays more than five dollars for anything."

"Then why did you ask so much?" Bob demanded. "That was a tough-looking customer. He wasn't happy when he left."

"I know." Jupe started to explain. "I—I had a hunch something was wrong, that's all. I'm not sure why. I felt he wanted those bars too much. So I just stepped up the price to find out how much they really were worth to him."

"Well, you found out," Pete said. "Twenty dollars. And when your uncle finds out you turned down that much money, I'll bet he blows his top."

Jupe looked up and sighed. "We'll find out soon enough. Here comes Uncle Titus now!"

The large pickup truck rolled into the yard with Hans behind the wheel. As Titus Jones got down from the cab, Jupe noticed that the truck was empty.

"What happened, Uncle Titus?"

His uncle tugged at his long walrus moustache. "Seems as if there's been a run on iron bars lately. Guess I got to the place too late. Every last one of them was gone."

Jupe cleared his throat. "Aunt Mathilda already sold that batch you bought yesterday. And we just had another customer looking for some, too."

"That so?" his uncle asked. He dug out his pipe and lit it. "Well, no mind. We'll get some more in some day."

Jupe moved his feet uneasily. "This customer wanted to buy those last few bars, the ones for the cages. He was willing to buy them with or without the cages."

His uncle looked at him. "Buy the bars without the cages? How much did he offer?"

"Twenty dollars," Jupe replied, swallowing hard.

"Twenty dollars?" Titus thought about it. "What did you tell him?"

"I said it wasn't enough. That we didn't want to sell the bars alone. That we were planning to fix up the cages to sell to the circus."

Titus Jones rocked back and forth, blowing smoke. "How much did you ask him for the cages?"

Jupe took another deep breath. "A thousand dollars," he said, waiting for the explosion. The only response was more smoke as Titus Jones puffed silently away. "A thousand dollars apiece," Jupe added slowly. "Four thousand for the lot."

His uncle removed the pipe from his mouth. As Jupe waited for the expected tongue-lashing, a car swung into the yard. It came to a quick, jarring stop near them. A man stepped out.

"That's him," Jupe said.

The hatchet-faced man walked up. "You the owner of this junkyard?" he demanded.

"I am," Mr Jones said.

"My name's Olsen." The visitor jabbed his finger in Jupe's direction. "Fine help you leave when you're away. I tried to buy some of your old junk bars and this kid tried to scalp me."

"That so?" Mr Jones asked in a matter-of-fact voice. "Sorry to hear about it, mister."

The man grinned. "I thought you would be."

He took out his wallet and extracted a twenty-dollar note. "I offered him twenty dollars for those bars over on that pile and he turned me down flat."

Titus Jones inclined his head towards the pile the man indicated. "Aint no bars there, mister. Just some old animal cages."

"I know," Mr Olsen said impatiently. "But I don't need the cages. Just the bars." He extended the money to Titus Jones. "Here you are—twenty dollars. Is it a deal?"

Titus Jones relit his pipe and puffed hard to get it going properly. Jupe waited. The man stirred restlessly.

"Sorry, mister," Titus said at last. "But my nephew here told you the truth. Those bars you're talking about there are for animal cages. When we get 'em fixed up nice and proper, I figure on selling them to the circus for their animals."

Jupe stared at his uncle. Pete and Bob stood open-mouthed.

Mr Olsen scowled. "Okay—animals cages. Do you know what he wanted for the four of them? Four thousand dollars! He asked a thousand dollars apiece!"

"Well," Titus said, "the boy's young, and he did make a mistake quoting the price."

"I thought so," the man said, smiling with satisfaction.

"The price is six thousand dollars," Titus Jones said. "That would come to fifteen hundred dollars apiece."

The visitor stared. Titus Jones put his pipe in his mouth, puffed, and rocked on his heels. Once more Jupe held his breath, waiting for Mr Olsen to explode.

At that moment Hans walked up. "Anything else I can do, boss?" he asked Mr Jones. "I still got time to do some cleaning up."

Mr Olsen looked at the hulking figure of the yard helper. His cold eyes flickered. Then he snarled. "Forget it, mister. I've got better use for my money."

Jupiter watched the saloon roar out of the yard. He felt like hugging his uncle.

A few minutes later, The Three Investigators were crawling through the big pipe leading to Headquarters. As soon as they were inside, Jupe squinted into the See-All periscope, which let him see over the piles of junk outside the trailer.

"All clear," he reported. "Mr Olsen hasn't returned."

"Gosh!" Bob exclaimed. "You could have knocked me over with a feather when your Uncle Titus backed you up."

"Six thousand dollars!" Pete said. "And I thought that *you* were off your rocker!"

Jupiter nodded. "I don't blame you, Second. But Uncle Titus has an affection for the circus that goes far beyond his usual desire to do business and make a reasonable profit."

"What beats me," Bob said, "is why everyone wants to buy bars all of a sudden?"

"You should have asked your Aunt Mathilda who the other buyer was—the one who bought up the whole lot," Pete said to Jupe.

Jupe was about to reply when the telephone rang.

"Hello, Jupiter Jones speaking."

They could all hear the incoming voice through the loudspeaker attachment. "Hi, Jupe. This is Mike Hall. How would you fellows like to come back to our place again tonight?"

"I don't know if we can get away, Mike," Jupe said. "Why—is anything wrong at Jungle Land?"

"Not exactly," Mike said. "I just thought you'd like to see the gorilla. He just arrived."

"Swell," Jupe said. "Is he a big one?"

Mike laughed. "Big enough. Of course, he'll keep, but our big problem is still with George. And I hope you remember that he gets nervous after dark."

"We haven't forgotten, Mike. As a matter of fact, we were discussing that same point—that we don't know yet what goes on there after dark."

"Well, here's your chance to find out," Mike said cheerfully.

"All right, Mike. We'll try to get permission, and then it'll be just the matter of arranging transport."

"Great," Mike said. "I can meet you at the gate. You coming by pickup truck again?"

"I don't think so," Jupe replied. "This time I believe we'll be using the Rolls."

There was a gasp. "You have a Rolls-Royce?"

64

Mike asked. Then he began to laugh loudly.

"Ask him what's so funny," Bob said.

"I heard that," Mike said. "It's funny because Mr Jay Eastland acts like such a big shot, you know. And that's the car he drives to impress people."

Jupe consulted his watch. "We'll be there about nine, Mike, after dinner. As soon as I call Worthington."

"Worthington? Who's he?"

"Our chauffeur."

There was loud laughter from the other end. "Wow!" Mike managed to say finally. "Okay, see you later."

Jupiter replaced the phone. "I guess I should have explained to Mike we don't actually own the Rolls and Worthington."

"It's better this way," Bob put in. "At least we cheered him up. The way things are going at Jungle Land, he needs a laugh."

Promptly at nine o'clock that evening, the gleaming old Rolls-Royce rolled up to the main gate at Jungle Land.

Jupe peered out of the window. "I thought Mike said he would meet us here."

There was an overhead light illuminating the gate area. Beyond that, Jungle Land was dark. Palm leaves rustled in the night breeze. From the distance came strange chattering sounds.

Pete jumped out and opened the gate. As the Rolls passed through, he closed it again and got back into the car. "I'm glad Worthington is driving us in," he said. "This place is kind of scary at night."

Following Pete's unerring sense of direction, Worthington threaded his way through several junctions and side roads. As he was about to turn up the road leading to the big white house on the hill, Pete touched the dignified chauffeur's shoulder. "Hold it a second, Worthington."

Jupe raised his eyebrows. "What's up, Pete?"

"I thought I heard shouting up ahead—and some other noises."

They waited, concentrating on listening. Soon they all heard sounds in the undergrowth. Then they heard the faraway wail of a siren.

Bob pointed into the dark. "Look! Searchlights!"

As their eyes watched the blue arcs of light sweeping the skies, they became aware of crashing sounds directly ahead of them. They heard the rasp of heavy breathing. In the next instant, a figure broke out of the jungle. The headlights of the Rolls picked him out clearly as he ran across the road.

His eyes were wide and staring. Sweat glistened on the dirt-streaked face under the old Aussie campaign hat. There was no mistaking the man caught for a brief moment in the bright headlights.

"Hank Morton!" Bob exclaimed.

"Running wild through the woods—and looking mighty scared," added Pete. "I wonder what he's been up to now."

The panting man plunged into the thick jungle on the other side and disappeared. The crashing sounds of his flight gradually diminished.

They heard angry cries up ahead, and saw the beams of bobbing torches.

"It looks like some kind of trouble," Bob said, peering out.

"Let's see what's going on," Jupe cried.

In a moment the boys were scrambling out and running. A voice called out.

"Jupiter! Bob! Pete!"

Jupe turned, peering uncertainly into the darkness.

A torch signalled. "Over here. It's me—Mike."

He directed them with the torch until they were together. Jupe noticed Mike was breathing hard. Behind him, dim figures were walking slowly through the jungle, swinging torches from side to side, and then up towards the trees. A few men were holding rifles.

Jupe caught his breath as he took in the eerie scene. "What's going on?" he asked. "Did George break out again?"

"It's not George this time," Mike said breathlessly. "It's a lot more trouble than that."

"What happened?" asked Bob. "Some of those men have rifles. Are they looking for Hank Morton?"

"Who?"

"Hank Morton," Pete said. "We just saw him running scared. He broke out of the jungle below the hill and ran across the road."

"So that's it!" Mike Hall said grimly. "I knew it!"

"Knew what, Mike?" Bob demanded. "What's going on here?"

"The gorilla I told you about," Mike began. "He broke out of his cage and escaped!"

"When?" Pete demanded. "You mean there's a wild gorilla running loose here?"

"It happened a little while ago, right after Doc Dawson brought George home this evening."

"A wild gorilla and a lion," Jupiter said thoughtfully. "I don't know much about how those two species get along, Mike. Would a gorilla be that frightened at the presence of a lion that he would break out of his cage?"

Mike shrugged. "Jim knows more about that than I do. But after what you told me, I'm not at all sure he did break out of his cage."

"What do you mean, Mike?" asked Pete.

"I mean somebody could have let him out. Somebody who hated my Uncle Jim bad enough to pull a stunt like that. You said yourselves you saw him running through the woods.

"Unless I'm dead wrong, it was Hank Morton who let him out!" he said bitterly.

10

In the Dark

JUPE shook his head. "Hank Morton could have been running through the woods for any number of reasons. That's not proof that he let your gorilla escape. Perhaps if we could see its cage, we might find some clues."

"Okay, you fellows are the investigators," said Mike. "Maybe you'll discover something." He led them up the hill. "Say, where's that Rolls-Royce you said you were coming in?"

"Down at the foot of the hill," said Bob. "Worthington is used to us. He'll just wait until we show up again."

Mike chuckled and brought the boys to a clearing at the side of the house. Lights blazed in every room, lighting up the nearby area. Mike pointed and The Three Investigators found themselves staring at a large, empty cage.

"The shipment arrived not long after you left this afternoon. There were two cages this time and—"

"Two cages?" Jupe asked.

A snarling, spitting sound behind him made him whirl in fright. Bob and Pete flinched.

"Gosh!" Bob gasped. "What was that?"

69

Mike directed his flashlight to the far end of the house. "I guess I should have warned you first. Take a look! Isn't that a beauty?"

The boys looked in awe at the sinister creature caged barely twenty feet from them. As they slowly approached, it snarled again.

"It's a black panther," Mike said. "How do you like it?"

Gleaming yellow eyes stared unwinkingly at them from behind thick iron bars. As they took another cautious step forward, the panther hissed. Its mouth opened, showing long, white pointed fangs. Hastily, the boys stepped backward.

Bob gulped. "I like him fine. Just so long as he stays locked up in that cage."

"Wow!" Pete exclaimed. "Look at those muscles! If you ask me, that panther looks a lot tougher than old George."

As if acting in support of Pete's observation, the beast snarled and lunged at the bars with a frightening thud. The boys retreated another step, watching the black animal warily.

"It would be a pretty good fight, at that, Pete—lion against panther," Mike said. "Panthers, this kind, are really leopards. They strike like lightning. They've got terrible raking claws as well as sharp teeth. But don't let George fool you with his dumb, gentle act. He's still a lion—a good-sized one at that—over four hundred pounds—and he's simply too big and powerful for the panther. No panther ever beat a lion yet, that I ever heard of. It would take a tiger to do it."

The boys stared in silence at the animal pacing restlessly in its cage. "I kind of agree with Pete," Bob said finally. "This baby looks real mean and tough. What do you think, Jupe?" He looked around. "Jupe?"

The First Investigator was spotted by the cage the gorilla had escaped from. He motioned them over.

"What's up, Jupe?" asked Bob.

"This cage has been tampered with, fellows," Jupe announced. "While I'm not certain that Hank Morton was responsible for the gorilla getting out, somebody was!"

"How can you tell?" asked Pete.

Jupe pointed dramatically to the side of the cage. "See there? One bar has been removed. The adjoining two are bent. The bars are set approximately six inches apart. I think whoever removed the bar gave the gorilla his chance. He bent the other two far enough apart to slip out. You said he was a big one? How big?"

"He wasn't full size, but big enough," Mike said. "About our size." He shook his head as they appraised each other. "Don't let the size fool you. He's twice as powerful as a grown man."

"Where did he come from?" Jupe asked.

"Rwanda, in Central Africa. We were expecting a young gorilla from there. We've been waiting a long time. Uncle Cal went through all the mountain gorilla terrain—Rwanda, the Congo, and Uganda. He finally wrote to us from Rwanda that he had a gorilla, but he was having trouble

71

getting it out of the country. Gorillas are on the endangered species list—there aren't very many of them left—and only zoos and scientists can get export permits for them. It took Uncle Cal a while to convince the authorities that Jungle Land was a kind of zoo."

"Gee," said Pete. "Wouldn't it have been easier to just get another kind of gorilla?"

"Well, there are lowland gorillas, but there's an embargo on them, too. I'm not even sure which species Uncle Cal finally sent us."

"It was a young male mountain gorilla," said a voice from the darkness. Jim Hall stepped out of the shadows and nodded to the boys.

"Have you found him yet?" Mike asked.

Jim Hall shook his head. His face was tired and dust-stained. "I just heard he's been seen up by the canyon. I wanted to check back here again before heading out."

"What happened with Mr Eastland?" Jupe asked. "Did George really attack Rock Randall?"

Jim Hall laughed harshly. "That was hogwash. It seems Randall got into a fight with somebody and got thrown around on some rocks on the movie set. He was beat up and bloody, and it did look as if George might have mauled him. But a doctor looked him over and said no animal could have made those marks. So we're clear of that mess, and now we have another. I'm glad you're back tonight, boys. You can see for yourselves that Alfred Hitchcock wasn't exaggerating when he told you something's wrong at Jungle Land."

There were shouts in the distance, and Jim Hall made an impatient gesture. "Sorry, boys, but I've got to get moving and trap that gorilla before something happens."

"I guess he'd be pretty dangerous to run up against," Pete ventured.

"He might be frightened now by all the racket out there. But if you happen to run into him, don't worry. Just get out of his way."

Bob blinked. "What? Meet a gorilla face to face and not worry? How do you manage that?"

Hall laughed. "I'll tell you something about gorillas. It applies to a lot of wild animals generally. Gorillas almost never behave aggressively. Oh, they bluff a lot, and scream and charge—that's how they frighten away any animal that seems threatening. But mostly gorillas are peaceful animals that mind their own business. They graze in the same area as elephants, for example, and although they eat the same food, there's no problem."

"What happens?" asked Bob.

The tall man shrugged. "Mutual disregard," he said. He glanced at his watch. A horn sounded. "That'll be Doc." He waved and walked away.

A moment later he passed, driving an open jeep. The thin, moustached man sitting next to him was holding a rifle.

Mike smiled. "It figures good old Doc Dawson would be around to help. He's crazy about animals."

Pete turned to look at the jeep carrying the two

men off. They looked prepared for action.

"If he likes animals all that much, why is he holding a rifle?"

"That's a stun gun," Mike said. "It shoots a tranquilliser dart—not bullets. Whatever is hit is only knocked out temporarily, Pete—not really hurt."

"Jim Hall and the search party should be able to find the gorilla," said Jupiter. "I suggest we look around now while we have the opportunity. Perhaps we can learn what's behind these animal escapes. First there was George, and now the gorilla."

"Well, George seems okay now," Mike said. "He's in the house sleeping off the tetanus and tranquilliser shots Doc Dawson gave him. Doc cleaned up the wound and George will be able to face the camera tomorrow and earn a day's pay for us."

Jupiter was looking round. "Does George have a cage, too?"

"No, we got rid of George's cage over a month ago," said Mike. "He sleeps in the house with Jim and me. He has his own room but he prefers to share Jim's."

Jupe glanced up at the lighted house. "You said somebody must have let him out before. Couldn't it happen again?"

Mike put his hand in his pocket and produced a key. "This time the house is locked. Only Jim and I have keys."

Jupe pondered. "You've told us, Mike, that

George becomes nervous and restless at night. I suggest we walk round to see if we can't uncover some reason for his nervousness. We should explore the area closest to the house to begin with."

"Swell," Mike said. "As you can see, the house is set in a clearing on this knoll. Over there s a shed for tools and firewood. It could be a garage but Jim parks outside here. The road at the foot of the drive leads north and runs into other roads."

He led the boys around the area. The night was quiet after the earlier excitement. The moon was now up, and the sky was cloudless.

Jupe nodded as if satisfied when they completed their circuit of the house. They returned to the cage area. The gorilla cage remained empty. The panther in the other lay quietly, switching its long tail and watching them balefully.

The Three Investigators followed Mike down the hill into the jungle. "I'll explain Jungle Land as we go along. Then the next time you come, you'll know your way around here without me."

"How big is Jungle Land?" asked Bob. "It seems with so much land to cover, you'd never know what's going on."

"It's about a hundred acres, and diamond-shaped. That's a lot maybe, but we've never had any trouble keeping track of things before."

"Where is the Jay Eastland movie being shot?" Pete asked.

"North of here, about a five-minute ride," Mike

said. "We're heading due east now, towards our closest border fence."

The trail descended steeply through brush, rocks and fissures. Faint patches of moonlight showed between trees.

"Where's the canyon your uncle said the gorilla was seen at?" asked Bob. "He seemed to be heading north, too."

"He was, but he'll cut left on another road. The canyon is north-west, about fifteen minutes away. Just below it, we have several acres that look like the African veldt, grassy and flat. We have the elephants there, contained by a moat, so they can't get out. But you can hear them trumpeting." He grinned. "I like that sound."

"I like it better myself now," said Pete, "knowing they can't get out."

Mike continued to describe Jungle Land as they went on downhill. "At the far west end opposite us is the built-up tourist section. Our main attraction used to be the jungle and animals, but a lot of folks seem to prefer the Wild West. So we have a frontier town, a mock graveyard, a ghost town, and a stagecoach ride for the kids. We keep the horses pretty near that area.

"In the southern part is the entrance where you come in, and lots of jungle. In the central part is the lake and then above that, where Eastland is, more jungle. At the northern end are mountains, with one high precipice. It's been used for a lot of movies where the hero has to dive off a cliff. Doc Dawson has his dispensary up that way."

There was an outburst of chattering cries and hoots. The boys stopped and looked at their guide.

"Those are monkeys and owls," Mike explained. "We've also got a snakehouse in the north-east section but the snakes don't make any noise. We keep them farthest away because they're the hardest to find in case they ever get away. We've a good collection of sidewinders—they're rattle-snakes—and a water moccasin and a good-sized king snake."

Jupe was peering intently back through the trees. "How far are we from your house now, Mike?"

"About five hundred yards. There's a fence down the end of this slope here—"

"Wait!" Pete whispered. "What's that?"

They all heard it then. A slow, dull, crunching sound echoing with a measured beat. The Three Investigators looked at each other. The crunching sound became louder, seeming to come closer. Prickly chills ran down their spines. Then they heard a new sound. It started as a low whine and began to rise on a shrill, insistent note.

"I don't like that," Pete said hoarsely. "Maybe we ought to be getting back—"

Jupiter's eyes were wide with fear, too, but they were also puzzled. "That sound—" he started to say. "It—it's—"

As he groped for words, the shrill, whining noise ascended to a full-noted shriek. The screech-ing seemed to be all around, engulfing them.

EEEE—ooo—EEEEE! EEE—ooo—EEEEE!

Bob yelled, "I'm getting out of here!"

With one mind, The Three Investigators wheeled and ran.

"Wait!" Mike called.

They turned to stare in utter amazement.

Mike Hall was laughing.

"It's nothing to worry about," he called. "That's only the *metal shredder!*"

II

Steps into Terror

THE shrill, wailing sound slowly fell until it became a low, whistling note.

"Metal shredder?" Jupiter repeated dumbly.

Mike was pointing ahead through some trees. "Yes, Jupe. Over the fence, the other side of our property. There's a salvage yard—steel and scrap iron. It's full of scrapped cars and other junk."

"What does the metal shredder do—besides scare people?" Bob asked.

"It's a new recycling process to salvage precious metal," Mike said. "Part of the new ecology drive. The cars used to be just pounded down and sold as scrap iron and steel. But now they have this new device—some kind of claw with a computer-selector-processing operation. It shreds the cars into little bits. The metal is separated from the other material, and then the more precious metals, like copper, are separated from the iron and steel."

"Whew!" Pete exclaimed weakly. "Is that all? It sounded like all the gorillas in town were holding a convention!"

Jupe was plucking at his lower lip. He glanced at his wristwatch.

"It is now nine thirty," he stated. "Does George usually become nervous and restless about this time, Mike?"

Mike shrugged. "Sometimes sooner or later. I don't know exactly what time—except that it's always after it gets dark."

"Always at night? Never during the day?"

"Never," Mike said firmly. "But I'm not counting this afternoon. George wasn't nervous then—just acting mean. I'd say because he was hurt."

"What's your idea, Jupe?" Bob asked. "That the sound of the metal shredder made George nervous?"

"Animals are more sensitive to sounds than humans," Jupe said. "Perhaps George is reacting to that high whine of the metal shredder."

"But he'd hear it all the time then," Pete put in. "Not just at night."

"A good point. Second," said Jupe, "does this metal-shredding process operate during the day, too, Mike?"

"Sometimes," Mike said. "Off and on again. I

don't pay much attention to the sound any more. It isn't nearly as loud up by our house."

"Hmmm," Jupe said. "How long has that machine been in operation?"

"It's kind of new, Jupe. The scrap yard has been here a long time, a number of years. And the wrecking part of it, also. But offhand my guess is they haven't been using this metal shredder more than a month."

"A month," Jupe repeated. "And how long has George been acting nervous and restless?"

"Since about two or three months ago," Mike said. "I remember it started just before the rainy season when Jim decided to bring George inside the house for good."

Jupiter scowled, puzzled.

"Don't forget, he didn't act up every night," Mike added. "He was restless at times, then seemed to be all right. But the last week or so, he's been getting much worse, and it's been regular since."

"So he was nervous before the metal shredder came in," Bob said.

Jupe looked thoughtful. "It would seem that George isn't used to being cooped up indoors at night. That might account for his actions. The metal shredder could be a factor, or perhaps not. There could be different reasons."

"Maybe it's working in the movie that's making him nervous," Pete suggested, grinning. "A lot of actors get nervous at night trying to memorise their lines for the next day's shooting."

Jupiter snapped his fingers. "A humorous

suggestion but nevertheless a possibility, Pete." He turned to Mike. "How long have Jay Eastland and his crew been working at Jungle Land?"

"They've been around here about two months," Mike said. "But a lot of that time was spent checking the locations, getting the setups planned for the shooting scenes, the right backgrounds, and so forth. They didn't move in completely and start shooting until two weeks ago."

"Do they shoot at night, too?" Jupe asked.

"Sometimes."

Jupe frowned. "You said their set is about five minutes away from your house. Would their mikes pick up the sound of the metal shredder?"

"It's possible," Mike admitted. "I don't know. Mr Eastland hasn't complained."

"He might not have to do his sound work at Jungle Land," said Pete, drawing on information he'd picked up from his father. "Sometimes the sound is dubbed in later—even the actors' voices."

Jupe nodded. "What about the actors and work crew? Do they live here, too?"

"Most of them go home at night," Mike said. "The motorway is near here and most of them don't live too far away—Westwood, Hollywood, West Los Angeles—it's only a half-hour ride."

"What about Mr Eastland?" Jupe asked. "Does he stay here?"

"He can. He has his own trailer out there, and one apiece for the two stars, Rock Randall and Sue Stone. Uncle Jim rented them all of Jungle Land so they can stay if they want to. The gate is open and they come and go as they please. I don't check and neither does Jim."

"But they could be here," Jupe said stubbornly. "They could be snooping around your house at night and making George nervous."

"Why would they be doing that, Jupe?" asked Bob.

"I can't think of any sensible reason, Bob," he said. "All I say is the possibility exists."

"Let's get on with the tour, fellows," said Mike. "Come on down to the fence and then we'll circle around to the other side of the house."

As the boys approached the fence, the strange sounds from the scrap yard began again. The rhythmical crunching, grinding noises ebbed and then the wailing sound started. This time the boys were expecting the almost human shriek of the mechanism and remained calm.

"Happy metal shredding!" Bob said, holding his ears. "I'm surprised *all* your animals aren't nervous wrecks!"

Jupe looked at the fence gleaming in the moonlight. Metal stakes were pegged into the ground several yards apart, supporting a netting of wire links.

"Does this fence run all the way along your property line, Mike?" he asked.

"Yes," Mike said. "It continues north past the salvage yard. Then there's a big drainage ditch behind it which runs parallel the rest of the way. The fence is six feet high all the way, like it is here, and is strong enough to keep practically all our animals from escaping if they should happen to get loose."

The boys continued north along the fence and then began to cut back up the hill through trees and tall grass. Suddenly Pete stopped.

"What's up, Pete?" Bob said.

The tall boy pointed unsteadily ahead.

"Did you hear that?" Pete whispered.

The sounds from the salvage yard had ceased for the moment, and the boys all stood still, listening hard.

"Where, Pete?" asked Jupe. "What is it?"

Pete pointed again. "There."

They heard a rustling sound in the tall grass and then heavy breathing.

"*There!*" Pete whispered hoarsely again.

The others followed the line of his keen sight. As they stared into the jungle darkness, they saw a shadowy movement.

They froze, scarcely daring to breathe.

Something moved from behind a tree.

It came forward, moving in a peculiar way. Then they saw the dark head, swaying between hunched, shaggy shoulders.

Jim Hall had told them they would be in no particular danger. Somehow they could not believe it as the panting gorilla came closer!

12

Noises in the Night

JUPITER recovered his senses first.

"Run!" the stocky leader of The Three Investigators shouted. "Ramble and scramble!"

The three turned and ran. Mike hesitated, torn between flight and duty. He stared a moment longer at the oncoming gorilla. Red-rimmed eyes glowered at him from beneath the shaggy, beetling brows.

Jupe, glancing back, saw the situation. "Run, Mike! He might be dangerous now!"

The creature raised its long arms and bared yellow teeth. Mike, with a sharp intake of breath, wavered, then broke and ran to join the others.

The gorilla pounded its chest, veered, and disappeared into the high grass.

"Where'd he go?" Bob called.

"He's in the grass. I think we scared him off," cried Mike. "Come on—I think we'd better head for the house."

Warily they circled the area, their hearts pounding. They were nearly at the crest of the incline when suddenly the grass parted in front of them. Too late, they saw the shaggy creature step out.

The boys stood frozen with fear. The hulking creature raised its heavy arms and opened its mouth. A strange sound issued from its throat.

"Hit the ground!" a voice called sharply.

As the boys dived to the side, they heard a dull, thudding sound. They looked up to see Jim Hall and the vet with his stun gun raised.

The gorilla swayed, a puzzled look on its dark face. Then it moaned and toppled heavily to the ground.

"You boys all right?" Hall asked. They nodded dumbly, still shaken. "Nice shooting, Doc," he said.

The vet nodded without changing expression. He walked up quickly and stood over the fallen gorilla as it feebly moved its limbs.

"He's not hurt," he told the boys as they crowded round. "It just takes a few seconds for the tranquillising drug to take effect. Then he'll have a nice long sleep and we'll be able to get him back to his cage."

"Looks like we circled back in time," Jim Hall said, frowning. "Somebody sent us off on a wild goose chase to the canyon for nothing. He could have been hiding in the trees here all the time."

"Who told you the gorilla was in the canyon?" Jupe asked.

"Jay Eastland," Hall said tersely.

Doc Dawson leaned over the inert simian. "He's out already, Jim. Give me a hand and we can lug him to the car."

Hall stooped and deftly roped the gorilla. He

and Doc dragged the unconscious animal off. The boys followed as the two men hoisted it into the rear of the open jeep.

"Where are you taking him now, Mr Hall?" Jupe asked.

"Back to his cage. Let's hope he stays put this time."

"Uncle Jim," Mike put in, "Jupe noticed that one of the cage bars was missing. The ones next to it were bent, so that's how he got out."

Hall glanced keenly at Jupiter. "That's how it happened, all right. Sure looks like somebody is trying to sabotage us, doesn't it?"

"It would appear so, sir. But now I'm wondering how you can put the gorilla back into that cage and expect him to stay there."

"That's easy," Hall said. "There's a man at work now replacing the missing bar and straightening the bent ones."

The jeep nosed out along the trail and Jupiter and the others followed at a dogtrot. Workmen were busy at the gorilla's cage when they arrived at the house.

A large man with close-cropped hair turned to face them. His arms were thick and muscular, one of them heavily tattooed. He held a long hammer in one hamlike hand.

"She's all set now," he said to Jim Hall. He glanced at Doc Dawson. "Got him already? That was fast work, Doc."

Jim Hall strode forward to the cage and the burly helper stepped aside. Hall put his weight against the cage bars, gripping them tightly and jerking his body from side to side.

"Okay. That ought to hold him, Bo. Thanks." He turned to the jeep. "Better give us a hand here with Kong."

"Sure thing," the man said, tossing down his hammer.

"Hold it a second!" Doc Dawson said. "I want to check out that cage myself. I've got enough to do without running around day and night looking for lost animals."

The helper shrugged and grinned. "Sure, Doc. You want us to lock you up inside and then see if you can get out?"

"Very funny, Jenkins," Dawson snapped.

He came forward and picked up the heavy hammer. He slowly tapped each bar on the empty cage. He bent forward attentively as if he were listening for a flaw in the metal. Then he grabbed the bars in his strong, weatherbeaten hands, tugging and twisting, applying pressure from all sides.

"Satisfied?" Bo Jenkins asked.

"Seems okay," Doc Dawson growled. "Those bars stand up to me all right, but then I don't have the strength of a gorilla." He looked at Bo Jenkins coldly. "Reckon you don't either, Bo. But if you're taking Hank Morton's place here, you can't afford to make any mistakes!"

Jim Hall turned to Doc Dawson. "Bo is working out fine, Doc. You're the one who told me he could take Hank Morton's place and do a good job, and I'm satisfied so far. Why needle him?"

"Just want him to be on his toes, that's all," Dawson said gruffly. "We don't want any more accidents around here." He stepped back to look at the empty gorilla cage again, and shook his head. "Darned if I can figure out how that bar got removed. I'd better check the panther's cage too."

Carrying the hammer, he walked abruptly to the cage opposite. The black cat leaped to its feet, hissing and snarling. The vet walked around the cage striking each of the bars in turn.

"He appears to be checking for a metal fault," Jupe said to his friends. "I've heard of something called metal fatigue. Airplane parts are checked for that periodically."

"With a hammer?" Bob asked.

Jupe shrugged. "Maybe Doc Dawson has his own method of detection. After all, he spends a lot of time with caged animals."

After several ringing blows, Doc Dawson stepped back and nodded as if satisfied. "Okay, Jim," he said. "Far as I can tell, the bars check out with equal resistance. No cracks or fissures, and they're all securely in place. I guess you can put the gorilla back in now."

Jim Hall signalled the work crew, who lifted the still-slumbering gorilla into its cage. Hall slipped the ropes off, swung the cage door shut, and padlocked it.

Doc Dawson stepped into his jeep. "Looks like you're all set now, Jim. I've got a sick horse to look after at the corral. If you need me again, just holler."

"Let's hope I don't, for a while, Doc. Thanks again for your help."

"Put it on the bill!" Dawson yelled. He waved and drove off.

Bob nudged Jupiter. "More fun coming," he whispered. "Here comes Jay Eastland."

The long station wagon roared up and the fat, bald-headed producer jumped out. Hall's lips tightened.

Eastland strode up quickly and peered into the gorilla cage. "So you got him finally, eh? Sure took you long enough, Hall. You had my crew scared out of their wits!"

"Yes, we got him," Jim Hall said slowly. "We might have caught up with him sooner, but somebody gave us a wrong tip. It turned out he wasn't in the canyon area at all but right around here, down by the fence."

The producer shrugged. "So what? I heard he was seen near the canyon and passed the word on to you." His voice rose. "How do you expect me to shoot a movie if you can't keep your wild animals under lock and key? My actors are worried sick that any moment they're going to be attacked by another one you let get away!"

"I'm sorry, Eastland," Hall said quietly. "We've had a few accidents, but nothing serious has happened. Everything's fine now and under control. You can tell your actors not to worry. Go on back and shoot your movie and leave us alone. You're only getting my animals stirred up and excited."

Eastland's face turned a mottled red. He backed up a few steps and shook his fist. "Don't tell me what to do, Hall. I've rented this place and—"

Suddenly there was an ear-splitting snarl from behind him. Eastland turned in alarm. The black panther leaped forward, and Eastland screamed in terror as the big cat crashed against its cage bars and fell back snarling.

The producer looked ill. His face was white and his eyes rolled. Then he noticed Jupiter and his friends watching.

"What are these kids doing here?" he barked. "What are you running—a sideshow?"

"They're here at my invitation, Eastland," said Jim Hall. "They've a job to do for me here. Now, is anything else bothering you?"

Eastland glowered. His chest rose and fell quickly. "Just make sure your animals don't get loose again, or you'll be sorry!"

Head down, he stamped away.

As the station wagon roared off, Jupe looked after it, puzzled. "That man certainly doesn't act like a movie producer, Pete. He acts—well—very unstable!"

Pete smiled. "He's what they call a 'quickie' producer in the trade, Jupe. They're hustlers, only interested in grinding out something fast and getting their money back even faster. If you ask me, Mr Eastland has money problems. So what he does is holler and bully and bluster."

"Speaking of noise," said Jupe, "we haven't heard the metal shredder for a while. Let's go back to the fence. I want to have another look round down there before we leave."

"I'd go with you, Jupe, but I've a lot of chores to do around here yet," Mike said. "I'll have to say good night."

Jupe glanced at his watch. "We'll have a quick look. And we'll try to come back tomorrow to continue our investigation."

With that, the stocky boy headed away from the house into the darkness. Pete and Bob shrugged and slowly followed.

"Here goes," Bob said. "We're off to test the sound barrier again. Remind me next time to bring along earmuffs."

"Remind me next time to stay home," Pete said. "I've had enough excitement tonight with that gorilla chasing us."

They walked down the slope and soon caught up with Jupiter. He was crouching behind a tree near the bottom.

"What—" began Pete, stopping when Jupe held up his hand.

Putting his finger to his lips, Jupe motioned them towards him. Quietly they stooped and scuttled over.

The metal shredder was quiet, but something else wasn't. They heard a dull thud, then a clanking noise. Then a crackling sound.

"In the salvage yard," Jupe whispered. "There's a man there. Tell me if he looks familiar."

Pete and Bob peered intently through the fence into the moonlit yard. Suddenly there was a flare as a man struck a match and held it to a cigarette. His sharp features were clearly seen.

"Hatchet-Face!" Pete whispered. "The man who came to the junkyard!"

"That's him, all right," Bob whispered. "He said his name was Olsen, didn't he? What's he doing here?"

"Listen," Jupe said.

They heard a crackling, sputtering sound.

The hatchet-faced man hunched over. Something dark glittered in his hand. His lips moved.

Again there was the sputtering sound.

"Walkie-talkie," Jupe said. "Hatchet-face is transmitting!"

13

Pursued!

"COME on," said Jupiter, "I want to hear this."

He pointed diagonally ahead to a clump of eucalyptus trees right by the fence. Their low-hanging branches would give good cover if the boys could get under them unobserved. Cautiously Jupiter wriggled forward, practically on his stomach. Pete and Bob slithered after him. Soon they were safely under the trees, enveloped by darkness and the oily, medicinal smell of the eucalyptus leaves. The boys peered out and found themselves staring at Olsen barely twenty feet away.

A metallic sputter came from Olsen's walkie-talkie. He bent to speak into it, and this time the boys could hear him clearly.

"Come on over this way," Hatchet-Face ordered.

His walkie-talkie crackled. "Okay," came the answer.

A dark figure was making his way slowly across the huge, disorderly pile of scrap. He held a walkie-talkie, too, with its long antenna extended.

The hatchet-faced man spoke. "Any luck yet, Dobbsie?"

The other shook his head as he slowly advanced, peering closely at the scrap metal under his feet. "Not a thing," he said, his voice filtering through Olsen's walkie-talkie.

"Stay with it," Hatchet-Face said. "It could be buried."

Olsen stooped and tossed an old mudguard aside. It fell with a dull clank. He repeated the action with a bumper and a radiator grill, scrutinised the area closely, and shook his head.

The other man drew closer, also lifting and discarding objects in his path. At last he came close enough to join Olsen. He was dressed like Olsen, in a dark business suit.

Both men pushed down their walkie-talkie antennas. "It's like looking for a needle in a haystack," the other man complained wearily.

"I know," Hatchet-Face said. "But we can't take the risk of losing it now. It's too big a haul to let get away."

"What about the other place?"

"The junkyard? Probably clean, but we'll have to keep an eye on it. The fat kid may be wise to something. We'll get back to him later."

Jupe and his companions exchanged glances. He was the only fat kid they knew of connected with a junkyard. Jupe swallowed. He didn't like being called fat. And he liked even less the threat in Olsen's last words.

The other grinned. His face was square and pale, centred by a flat, mashed nose under little beady eyes. "What about the two new ones Hall just got in? Shouldn't we go for those?"

Olsen shook his head. He reached into his pocket for a scrap of paper and looked closely at it. "Not yet. It would be too risky and our birds might fly away." He tapped the paper. "The information we got from Dora's alarm spells it out for us. DOX ROX NOX EX REX BOX. Six X's. It could be the cable code or else they're talking about six hundred K's. That's about half a million dollars, Dobbsie—not bad, at all. That's a lot of rocks."

The beady-eyed man shrugged. "Sure it is, and we might blow the whole deal by waiting. Why don't we just move in on him?"

Hatchet-Face replaced the paper in his pocket. "We wait," he said firmly. "He'll give us an opening. Somebody got careless tonight. If we can find the rocks first, we'll wrap them both up."

"Okay. You're running the show."

"You bet. I'm going up now to find out if Eastland has his finger in this. He's desperate for money and maybe he let the gorilla out for his own reasons. Remember, he'd have Hall on the hook for fifty grand if anything were to happen."

The other grinned and smacked his fists together. "I'd like a crack at Eastland. He ran me off the set."

Hatchet-Face laughed. "He won't bother me. Okay, Dobbsie, we check tomorrow same time."

Olsen waved abruptly and turned away. The other moved off in the opposite direction, across the salvage yard.

Pete nudged Jupe and pointed along the wire fence. The section towards which Olsen was heading had been tampered with. Where earlier it had been erect, it now sagged nearly to the ground.

As they watched, the hatchet-faced man carefully stepped over the lowered wire. He found a metal post and pulled it up straight, raising the wire along with it. That done, he wheeled, dusted his hands, and headed up the slope in the direction of the Hall house. Darkness covered him as he moved into the jungle. His footsteps could be heard for a while longer, and then they faded into silence.

The Three Investigators waited and then slowly got to their feet. The salvage yard was quiet, as if closed down for the night. The beady-eyed man had disappeared from view, too. The boys started back up the hill.

Pete suddenly hissed a warning and they froze.

They heard a stealthy movement in the grass and, as their pulses quickened, the sound of soft footsteps. Peering into the darkness of the jungle, they backed off uncertainly.

A thick, shadowy shape detached itself from a tree and stepped towards them. With hearts leaping, the boys turned and ran. A hidden root caught Jupe's foot and he fell heavily to the ground. His hand struck something hard and cold. He heard a growl behind him and grasped the hard object as he jumped to his feet. It was a length of metal pipe.

Pete grabbed Jupiter's arm and started to pull him along. There was an angry bellow from the darkness, and they were suddenly caught in the gleam of a torch.

Heavy footsteps crashed through the undergrowth. Still holding on to his weapon, Jupe fled, propelled by Pete. Bob was just ahead of them, his feet flying across the slope. He lost his footing and as he fell, Jupe and Pete charged into him, carrying him up and along.

The torch beam stabbed at them again, and they heard a harsh voice yelling for them to stop. Instead, they ran faster.

Panting noisily, following Pete's unerring sense of direction, the boys cut across the hillside. They burst out of the jungle on to the road to the Hall house. Just ahead was the gleaming Rolls-

Royce. As they ran for it, its headlights flicked on.

Jupiter flung the door open and threw himself inside.

"Quick! Step on it, Worthington!"

Bob and Pete tumbled in beside him as the tall chauffeur calmly answered, "Very good, Master Jones." The motor was already purring smoothly, and deftly he wheeled the big car round.

As they headed back for the exit gate, a man broke out of the jungle and leaped for the car. Worthington swerved instantly, and they had a brief glance at the contorted face of the man. He raised his fist and ran after them.

"Wow!" breathed Pete. "That's Bo Jenkins, the new animal helper."

Looking back through the glass, they saw Jenkins stop and shake his huge fist in a threatening gesture. It carried so much menace that they instinctively slumped low in the back seat of the car, although they were already safely away from their pursuer.

Pete jumped out as Worthington slowed down at the gate. He opened it, and after the car glided through, swung it closed again. Then Pete leaped back in and sat back, slowly shaking his head.

"What was that all about?" he asked.

Jupe had no reply. He could only scowl, puzzled as he gripped the weapon he had not used.

Pete, Bob, and Jupiter stood by the gates to The Jones Salvage Yard. Worthington had brought them back safely and had been thanked and dismissed.

"It's late," Jupiter said, "but I suggest we have a quick meeting. We have to put down what happened this evening between that man Olsen and the other, Dobbsie. It might contain clues we will need for solving this mystery."

He led the way swiftly into Headquarters, tossing the metal bar he had found at Jungle Land on to his work-bench before stooping to enter Tunnel Two. Inside, the boys clustered around the office desk, and Bob drew out his notebook.

"I take it we can skip the last part with that big guy Jenkins chasing us," said Bob. "There wasn't any mystery about that—he was just plain mad."

"We'll omit Bo Jenkins for the time being," Jupe agreed. "I imagine he was merely patrolling the property. Perhaps he was within his rights to chase off trespassers who might disturb the animals."

"I don't know about that," Pete protested. "We weren't exactly strangers there. He saw us earlier at the cage when Mr Hall and Doc Dawson brought the escaped gorilla back. He could have acted a lot nicer about it, if you want my opinion."

"True," Jupe said, "but it was dark. Perhaps he didn't see us clearly, and thought we were just some kids who had broken in. I'm inclined to give Bo Jenkins the benefit of the doubt. I suggest we ignore him and get to the discussion between Mr Olsen and Mr Dobbsie."

While Bob scribbled furiously, the boys reconstructed the conversation they had overheard and discussed what it might mean.

"What could be right under their feet?" asked Bob.

"It must be small," Pete said. "Because he also said it was like looking for a needle in a haystack."

"Not necessarily small," Jupe said. "It would be difficult to find something that looked like all the other junk in that heap."

"Like what?" asked Bob.

"I don't know," Jupe said. "But we have clues. Read back that part about rocks and X's, Bob."

"Okay," Bob said. "It went something like this: 'The information from Dora's alarm tells us. DOX ROX NOX EX REX BOX.' I assume all those words end in X because of the next bit. 'Six X's. Could be the code or six hundred K's. That's half a million dollars, Dobbsie. That's a lot of rocks.' "

"More or less correct, I believe," said Jupe. "Olsen also used the word 'cable'. We don't know who Dora is or what her alarm is, but Dora's message sounds like a cable. It's typical of what is called cablese—all the words are short and only important words are included. And, like many cables, this one seems to be in code. As a rule, parties who want to keep their business transactions secret establish a private code or cipher. Usually there's a key letter or word that lets them decipher each other's messages easily."

"Well, we don't have the key to the code," said Pete.

"I don't think we need one," said Jupe. "All those words probably end in X, as Bob said. But most of those words translate easily into plain English. The message can be read DOCKS ROCKS KNOCKS EX WRECKS BOX." He printed the decoded message for them on Bob's pad.

"Great," said Pete. "What's that supposed to mean?"

"I'm not sure," said Jupe, "but I'm getting an idea." He straightened up excitedly. "I think ROCKS is the important word. Olsen said something was half a million dollars, and then he said that was a lot of rocks. Does that suggest anything to you?"

"Half a million dollars worth of rocks?" asked Pete. "Rocks out of the ground? How's that possible? I mean, who'd want it?"

" 'Rocks' has another meaning, Pete," Jupe said. "It's also slang for 'money'. Olsen and Dobbsie are looking for money! Half a million dollars! My guess is that Olsen and Dobbsie are involved in some crooked scheme. They sound like gangsters, and that much money sounds like somebody's loot!"

"That's quite a guess," said Bob dubiously. "But even if that's true, what's the rest of the message supposed to mean?"

Jupe frowned. "I don't know, Bob. Apparently it tells where to find the money. Maybe the rest of the conversation will give us some clues."

"What about that part about wrapping them both up?" Pete asked. "Who's he talking about?"

Bob read from his notes. " 'If we can find the rocks first, we'll wrap them both up.' "

Jupe shook his head. "They spoke about one man first. They said, 'Why don't we move in on him?' Then later Hatchet-Face said, 'He'll give us an opening. Somebody got careless tonight.' "

"Who?" asked Pete.

Bob looked over his notes. "If being careless refers to letting the gorilla out, they think Eastland might have done it."

Jupe scowled. "I don't see why he would take such a risk. It's true that according to the agreement Jim Hall would have to pay Eastland fifty thousand dollars as forfeit for an accident. But I don't think Eastland would be foolish enough to take such a chance. That gorilla was dangerous! I'd sooner believe that Hank Morton was being spiteful again."

"Fine, but that has nothing to do with rocks," said Bob. "We're not getting anywhere."

Jupe tapped his fingers on the desk and thought awhile. "We're forgetting the first thing we ever learned about Olsen," he said finally. "He came here to the junkyard and wanted to buy cages. Then tonight he seemed to refer to me and the cages." Jupe winced as he remembered Olsen's calling him "the fat kid".

"Maybe he thinks he'll find his rocks in cages," said Pete sarcastically.

"Don't laugh," said Jupe. "Look! BOX in the cable might mean cage! WRECKS BOX means pull apart the cage and you'll find the money!"

"Your cages are already wrecked," objected Pete, "and Olsen didn't seem to think they were very valuable. He only offered you twenty dollars."

"True, true," said Jupe. "I can't explain that. But perhaps Olsen's really looking for another cage."

"Sure. In the scrap yard. Blending right in with the cars," said Pete. "I think we're all tired and just going round in circles."

Jupe stood up and stretched. "You're probably right, Pete. I suggest we quit for tonight. We haven't come to any definite conclusions—but at least we're sure of one thing."

"What's that?" asked Bob.

"We've got a mystery to solve," said Jupe with satisfaction.

14

Bob Makes a Discovery

THE next morning Bob came downstairs to breakfast more puzzled than ever. So much had happened the day before, and so little of it made any sense. He wondered if Jupiter wasn't grasping at straws in deducing the meaning of that crazy code.

Bob said good morning to his father, who grunted a reply from behind the morning newspaper. He was still on his first cup of coffee and obviously wasn't ready to talk to anyone yet. Bob looked around for something to read himself. He had read all the cereal boxes, so he turned to the stack of out-of-town newspapers lying on a nearby bookcase. His father, a newspaperman, frequently brought home papers from other parts of the country. He had explained to Bob that no one newspaper could carry all the news, and that he liked to see what stories other papers considered newsworthy.

Bob leafed idly through a paper, reading the comics and checking the headlines. He picked up another, and an article caught his eye. It was a UPI dispatch from Koster, South Africa. It read:

79-YEAR-OLD OPENS
AFRICA DIAMOND RUSH

With a whoop belying his 79 years, Pieter Bester leaped into the air, snatched his claim certificate, and took off running.

While 3,000 spectators cheered, he opened what could be the last official South African diamond rush, as 165 prospectors were turned loose Wednesday on the Swartrand alluvial diamond field.

Veteran prospector Hendrik Swanpoek, 72, who discovered the diamond field, had his usual luck. While staking out the first of his claims on the site, he unearthed a 48.12-carat diamond which he sold later for $42,000.

"I don't want to discourage anybody," Swanpoel said with a grin, "but I've already got most of the good stuff."

The article went on to give details of the government-sponsored diamond rush. The region was 75 miles northwest of Johannesburg, once known as the "Land of the Diamonds". In the uproarious boom days of 1927 and 1928, the article continued, 150,000 diggers scooped $28 million worth of high-quality gems from the Grasfontein and Bakerville diggings 50 miles west. The rules were, hopeful prospectors had their names put into a hat, and only the lucky ones whose names were drawn were permitted to the starting line. Each one was allowed three 45-square-yard claims. Veterans of earlier rushes hired local athletes for the sprint, or after careful coaching, had their sons run for them.

"Gosh!" breathed Bob. "Forty-two thousand dollars for one diamond! That's a lot of money!"

He turned the page and another news item caught his eye.

MAN INDICTED IN GEM CASE

Porto Ferraro, a former assistant to the Minister of Mines in Koster, South Africa, was indicted by a federal grand jury Tuesday on charges of smuggling diamonds into the United States last year. He was arrested at Los Angeles International Airport.

Customs agents found on his person five packages of cut and polished diamonds weighing a total of 659.14 carats, with a retail value of about $750,000. The two-count indictment charges Ferraro with smuggling and with failing to pay duty. Each count carries a possible sentence of two years in jail and a fine of $5,000.

"Wow!" said Bob. He'd never known diamonds were worth that much money.

"What's that?" said his father, putting down his newspaper and taking a sip of coffee.

"I was just reading about diamonds," explained Bob. "It says here that a 48-carat diamond sold for $42,000. That's a lot of money! What is a carat, anyway?"

"Well, it's a unit of weight used for gem stones. It's divided into 100 points, just the way a dollar is divided into 100 cents. A one-point diamond is very small. A 100-point, or one carat, diamond is a pretty good size."

"How big would that 48-carat diamond be, then?"

"Very large, for a diamond. Let's see, there was a famous Indian diamond called The Sancy. It was about the size and shape of a peach stone and weighed 55 carats. Your 48-carat diamond would be slightly smaller."

"How much would that weigh in pounds and ounces?"

"Here"—Mr Andrews pulled a reference book

out of the bookcase and handed it to Bob—"look up the table of weights and measures in this and see if you can figure it out."

Bob read that a carat was equal to 3.17 grains troy or 0.2 of a gram. A gram, the basic unit of weight in the metric system, equalled one twenty-eighth of an ounce. He scribbled some figures in his notebook and looked up in astonishment. "Forty-eight carats are only about one-third of an ounce."

His father nodded. "Yes, a carat is a very small unit of weight. You need a system with units that small when you're measuring such valuable things."

"Okay, how much is a carat worth?"

"No fixed amount. But for a diamond, you can figure roughly about a thousand dollars to a carat, depending upon the quality and brilliance of the stone. That 48-carat diamond sold for $42,000, you said. The gem was therefore not quite perfect, or a lot was lost in cutting."

"Cutting?"

Mr Andrews nodded. "Size and quality are important, but you can't evaluate a diamond until it's been cut into its usual 58 facets, and polished. Sometimes a lot is lost in the cutting process. You see, Bob, those found in diamond fields or mines are very rough stones, looking like ordinary rocks or pebbles—"

"Gosh!" Bob cried. "Excuse me, Dad! Thanks a lot—but I've got to make a phone call!"

Mr Andrews smiled as his son dashed off for the

phone. He was used to these abrupt endings to their conversations.

Bob quickly called Jupiter. "Hey, Jupe, did you know that uncut diamonds look like ordinary little rocks?" He went on to report what he'd learned from the newspaper and his father. "So maybe Olsen really is after rocks—diamonds!"

"Of course, of course!" said Jupiter. " 'Rocks' is also slang for 'jewels'." Jupiter was silent for a moment. "Good work, Records. Your information fits in very nicely with some further deductions I made this morning.

"Now, can you come right over here? Mike Hall called. George is acting a scene for Jay Eastland today and he'd like us to be there."

"Sure," said Bob, "but I thought you had to work today."

"Uncle Titus decided to stay home and work in the yard, so I'm not needed. Which is just as well. I have a strong feeling that things will continue to go wrong at Jungle Land until we solve its mystery. Meet me in Headquarters as soon as you can. Pete is already on his way."

"Konrad has offered to take us to Jungle Land today," Jupe was saying. "We've only a few minutes to discuss a serious problem that has come up. If my conclusions are correct, it may direct our actions when we get there."

Bob looked at Pete, mystified. "What's going on?"

Pete shrugged.

Jupiter announced importantly, "On the basis

of Bob's new information and my own deductions, I believe that the Hall brothers are involved in a smuggling racket!"

"What?" Bob protested.

Jupiter continued, "Cal Hall is shipping animals to his brother here. I think that under cover of those shipments he's also smuggling diamonds out of Africa."

Bob turned to Jupe. "But diamonds come from South Africa, and Cal Hall is operating in Central Africa. Aren't those two places a long way apart?"

"Mike told us that Cal Hall was in Rwanda for the mountain gorilla," Jupe said. "But for this kind of work, he would travel all over Africa. And there are a lot of other countries in Africa besides South Africa that produce diamonds. The Congo, Ghana, the Ivory Coast, Liberia, Sierra Leone, the Republic of Central Africa—all export diamonds."

He picked an atlas off a shelf and turned to a page showing Africa. "Here's a country in East Africa, not far from Rwanda. It used to be Tanganyika. See it? Right near Uganda and Kenya. It's called Tanzania now. It has diamond mines, too. Also, according to this atlas, the most abundant wild life is in East Africa. Cal has to get to the east coast to ship his animals, and he would naturally pass through Tanzania. If you note, there's a big coastal city. That's the capital, Dar es Salaam."

Pete whistled. "That sounds familiar. Get out your notes, Bob."

Bob whipped out his notebook and flipped to the page of the night before. " 'The information from Dora's alarm tells us,' " he read. He whistled. "Dora's alarm—Dar es Salaam—they sound pretty much the same."

"We don't yet know why Olsen should have that cable message," Jupe said. "But obviously Cal Hall sent it to his brother from the point of shipment, to let him know the diamonds were coming."

His eyes gleamed. "The first word of the cable makes sense now. DOX, spelled d-o-c-k-s, refers to a landing pier for ships. The diamonds and the animals are being shipped from the docks."

Bob printed out the two forms of the cable message on a clean piece of paper.

DOX ROX NOX EX REX BOX
DOCKS ROCKS KNOCKS EX WRECKS BOX

"We now think ROCKS means diamonds, and you think WRECKS BOX means to pull apart the cage," Bob said. "What about the other words?"

"I haven't figured out the third and fourth words yet," Jupe admitted. "But I think I was also incorrect about WRECKS. We should have left it as R-E-X, because that way everything falls into place!"

He paused significantly.

"C'mon, Jupe!" said Pete. "Out with it!"

"Rex is the Latin word for king. The lion is the king of beasts. REX BOX could mean, in this instance, George's cage! And George was shipped from Africa. I would say the message conclusively refers to smuggling diamonds into this country along with George and his cage. And, furthermore, I think the diamonds have become lost somehow, and whoever is looking for them is coming around too often—and making George nervous!"

Pete nodded. "Even an ordinary watchdog would be acting up if strangers were walking around at night near his house."

"But Jim Hall is no stranger," Bob protested. "And according to Jupe, he's part of the smuggling team."

"No, Jim Hall wouldn't make George nervous. It would have to be somebody else."

"Jay Eastland?" said Pete. "He'd get anybody upset."

"Well, I suppose he's a possibility," said Jupe. "But I can't see any connection at this point."

Pete snapped his fingers. "Hank Morton! I bet he's involved! Remember, he might have let George out the other day. He could have done it so that he could get a look at George's cage."

"You're forgetting George doesn't have his cage any more," said Jupe. "Remember Mike told us they got rid of it, and Jim allowed George to live in their house."

"What about Olsen and Dobbsie?" Bob asked. "Where do they fit in? They seem to know what they're looking for, and even where to look for it."

"Olsen and Dobbsie are definite suspects," Jupe said firmly. "They could be part of Jim's gang."

"Why are they looking in the scrap yard then?" Pete demanded.

"The diamonds could be lost there," Jupe said. "Remember what the man said—it was like looking for a needle in a haystack."

Bob flipped through his notes again and read, " 'They lost it and we'll wrap them up when we find it.' How do you explain that last part, Jupe? It doesn't sound like they're working with the Halls."

Jupe pondered. "I'd forgotten that part. According to that, Olsen and Dobbsie are against Cal Hall and Jim. The term 'wrap them up' suggests a threat, to me. Maybe Olsen and Dobbsie broke with the Hall brothers and are now trying to hijack the diamonds. Or perhaps they're a rival gang with no connection to the Halls."

"Gosh!" Bob said. "It all sounds complicated. I wonder if Mike knows anything about this."

"I doubt it," said Jupe. "And we must be careful not to accuse his Uncle Jim, whom he idolises, or his Uncle Cal, until we've made absolutely sure. Agreed?"

Bob and Pete nodded. Jupe got up and stretched.

"All right then. Konrad is waiting for us outside. Perhaps this trip will be the one in which we unravel the mystery at Jungle Land."

They walked to the exit glumly. They enjoyed solving mysteries, but solving this one seemed to entail making several people unhappy. Jupe bit his lip. He wondered how he would ever break the news to young Mike Hall.

15

Black Death

MIKE was waiting for The Three Investigators at his house when Konrad dropped them off. He guided them along a trail that served as a short cut to the location of the Jay Eastland movie set. It was a natural jungle setting, a flat clearing bordered by giant trees and thick undergrowth. Large rocks were scattered on the north side at the foot of a short but steep cliff. A ledge jutted out of the cliff a little way above the ground.

The movie set hummed with activity. The work crew was busy setting up cables and tall reflectors for the lights, which were set on huge iron tripods. Eastland was to one side, talking to a group of actors and checking their various positions while a few men pushed the camera into range.

Bob looked at the bustling workers. "Have they started yet?"

Mike shook his head. "It's been overcast all

morning. But the sun's coming out now and they'll start shooting any minute. George is in the first scene."

"Did he have a peaceful night?" Jupe asked. "Or was he nervous again?"

"He slept fine," Mike said. "He conked right out after Doc Dawson gave him the tranquilliser. A good thing, too, because that panther made a rumpus half the night."

"Oh, no," groaned Pete. "Don't tell me we have another mystery—a nervous panther!"

"I don't think so, Pete. He just needs to calm down from his trip and adjust to life here."

"How's George's wound, Mike?" asked Bob.

"Just about healed. You can barely even notice where he was cut."

Mike pointed to the edge of the set. Jim Hall stood alone with the big lion at his side. He saw them and waved them over. The Three Investigators walked up, cautiously watching George. The tawny beast sat quietly, its yellow eyes staring into the distance. Its long tail flicked as Hall rubbed its ears.

"Glad you could make it, boys," Jim Hall said. "As you can see, George is in great shape today. We've rehearsed his scene several times already, and he knows exactly what he's supposed to do." He glanced toward the busy producer-director. "I hope Eastland gets going soon while George is still nice and relaxed."

The big lion yawned, exposing long ivory teeth. A dull rumbling sound came from its throat.

As The Three Investigators looked up apprehensively, Jim Hall smiled. "He's purring, boys. That's a good sign. It means George is in a happy mood." He looked impatiently toward Eastland. "Come on, let's go," he muttered.

The fat producer moved across the set towards the cliff, giving instructions in a loud fretful, voice. "Over here with the camera," he ordered.

Eastland looked at a sheaf of notes. "We'll need to be on our toes for this scene. It's a quickie but we want to get it right the first time, understand?"

"No retakes makes it cheaper," Pete whispered in Jupe's ear.

Eastland waved an actress and an actor over. "Miss Stone, you and Rock Randall stand here." He pointed below the overhanging ledge. "The lion will be up on the ledge, looking down. You two will have a scuffle. When Randall has his back to the ledge, the lion jumps on him. Is that clear? Any questions, Sue? No? You, Rock? All right, then."

Eastland turned to the cameraman. "You hold on the scene as George jumps. Randall will try to fight him off, and they'll wrestle a few feet. Then Randall slumps to the ground, the lion paws him, and it's all over.

"We cut then to the next scene, which gives Hall a chance to come in and get his lion calmed down while we prepare the next setup with Sue. Hopefully, there won't be any trouble."

Jim Hall flushed. "George understands what

he's to do, Eastland. Just make sure Randall slumps to the ground and doesn't try to get up. If he does, George will knock him down again. There won't be any accidents."

The producer nodded with a smirk. "We all hope not." He turned to the actor. "I hope you've kept up your insurance policies, Rock."

The actor looked pale and frightened. "Come on, Jay. Cut the comedy."

He moved nervously away and lit a cigarette.

"Rock Randall looks awfully anxious," Jupe whispered to his friends. "And Eastland isn't helping him any by suggesting he can't trust George."

Pete looked at the big lion sitting placidly near its owner. "I don't blame Randall for looking nervous," he said. "How can you expect to be jumped by a big lion and not be nervous?"

"But he's trained," Mike said. "George won't hurt anybody. He'll only be pretending."

"I thought Rock Randall was in a fight yesterday," said Bob. "He doesn't look it."

"Make-up," said Pete knowledgeably.

Eastland walked across to the actress. "We'll shoot your scene with George right after that one, Sue. You'll be asleep in your tent. George pokes his head in the opening and goes in. He's just curious but you see him and wake up and scream. He opens his mouth and roars. That's it. Okay? You don't do anything silly like jumping out and hitting him. You just sit up, pull the covers up, and scream. You got it?"

The actress put her hand to her throat. "I've never worked with a lion before, Mr Eastland. Are you sure he's safe?"

Eastland smiled. He took a folded paper from his pocket and waved it. "That's what Jim Hall, his owner and trainer, says. I've got the guarantee down here in black and white."

The actress turned away, visibly upset.

Pete touched Jupe's shoulder and glanced away. Following his gaze Jupe saw the hatchet-faced man looking on from the edge of the set. He leaned forward to Mike. "That man over there, Mike—do you know him?"

"The thin-faced man—yeah—his name is Dunlop. He does some kind of work for Mr Eastland."

"Dunlop? Are you sure? Not Olsen?"

"It's Dunlop, all right. I've heard Eastland calling him that. I think he's some kind of technical expert on firearms."

Jupe glanced at Pete and Bob to see if they had overheard. They nodded. The man now identified as Dunlop walked casually away without looking back. Jupe frowned. He remembered that the night before the hatchet-faced man had threatened to return to The Jones Salvage Yard. Learning he was an expert on firearms made Jupe even less happy about it.

"How about Hank Morton?" Jupe asked. "Have you seen him around again?"

Mike grimaced. "He wouldn't dare to show his face around here again. We're just lucky Doc

Dawson got George in shape so fast for today's shooting."

"Say, Mike," said Jupiter, "what ever happened to George's cage? Where did you get rid of it?"

"I don't know. I suppose it was thrown over the fence into the scrap yard. That's where we throw most of our junk, and that cage was pretty old. Why?"

"Just curious," said Jupe.

Eastland suddenly snapped his fingers at Jim Hall. "Okay, Hall. We're all set. Get your lion up there and ready for action."

Jim Hall nodded and tugged gently at George's ear. "Come on, boy," he said softly. "We're putting you to work."

With George at his heels, he walked to the big rock formation. He stopped, leaned down, whispered, snapped his fingers, and pointed up to the ledge. George obeyed instantly and bounded lithely to the top. The lion stood there a moment, looking down majestically. It looked every bit its role of lord of the jungle, and Jupe and his friends gazed up at the animal admiringly.

Jim Hall whistled softly and gestured with his hand. The lion made a purring sound, then looked off into the distance, its long tail flicking restlessly.

Rock Randall and Sue Stone took their positions beneath the ledge. Eastland nodded. A man leaped forward. "Ready for action," he shouted. "Quiet on the set."

As all eyes focused on the impending action, Jupe caught his companions' attention and jerked his head to the side. He moved off quietly. Bob and Pete hesitated a moment, and then reluctantly followed.

"You picked a fine time to leave the set," Pete muttered when they were out of sight of the movie company. "Just when we finally had a chance to watch George act."

Jupe shrugged. "George's act is what I am depending on. I hope he has everybody's attention. That gives us a chance to do some investigating on our own."

"Where?" asked Bob.

Jupe pointed ahead in the direction of Jim Hall's house. "Diamond country," he said.

Cautiously, the boys approached the white house. "The new cages are around the other side," Jupe whispered. "I want to look them over first. It's quite likely that other cages besides George's are used for smuggling. We'll have to move quietly and make certain that we're not observed."

Bob looked surprised. "Observed by whom, Jupe? Everybody was around the movie set."

"Not everybody," Jupe said mysteriously.

Following Jupiter's example, Bob and Pete waited at the corner of the Hall house, listening. Then, they quickly moved round to the side, crouching low under the windows.

The two cages were separated by the length of the house. They approached the first one and peered in. "We're in luck," Bob said. "The gorilla's asleep."

The dark, shaggy form was huddled in a corner.

"What's so great about it?" Pete asked. "Are we going into its cage to look for smuggled diamonds?"

Jupiter moved slowly around the cage, examining it closely. "If diamonds are being smuggled in with these cages from Africa, how would it be done? Creating a false top or bottom seems a logical way, doesn't it?"

"Well, yes—" Bob agreed. "But can you tell just by looking?"

"No, it wouldn't be that obvious. The outside of this cage looks normal, the usual wood-frame roofing over the bars. But that seems too easy to get at. I've an idea the inside would be the more likely place. But for us to examine that thoroughly, the gorilla would have to be out of its cage."

Pete sighed with relief. "Thank goodness! I was afraid you'd want us to get in there with him."

Jupiter had already turned away. "Let's check the panther's cage," the stocky boy murmured. "Possibly we can detect someth—" He stopped suddenly and caught his breath.

Bob turned, puzzled. "What's wrong, Jupe?"

"Stay still!" Jupe hissed. "Don't make any sudden moves, and don't run!"

"What's going on?" asked Pete.

"Look straight ahead," Jupe said shakily. "The black panther's cage is open—and he's not in it!"

The boys stared at the empty cage. Prickly chills went down their spines and turned their legs to jelly. Then, horrified, they heard the sound they were dreading. A savage, spitting snarl behind them!

Jupiter gulped. He stood at a slight angle from Bob and Pete, and his quick sideways glance was enough to shake him further.

"H-he's up in the tree about twenty feet behind us," he whispered. "We may have to take a chance and separate. Now when I count three—"

Jupe's voice faltered as he saw the tall grass ahead of him ripple. He gasped as it parted and he caught the glint of a rifle barrel. Incredibly, he saw the rifle slowly rise.

A harsh voice directed, "Don't anybody move!"

The boys held their breath as a man stepped slowly out. They recognised the grizzled vet, Doc Dawson.

The grey eyes of the vet squinted. He took a slow step forward, his finger tightening on the trigger.

Suddenly there was an unearthly, ear-splitting scream behind them. In the same instant, the gun went off.

The boys ducked as a great, soaring shape smacked to the ground with a sickening thud a few feet past them. The black body twitched once and was still.

Doc Dawson stepped forward, looking both angry and discouraged. His dusty boot kicked at the long, outstretched claws of the panther.

"Lucky for all concerned I'm a pretty good shot," he said.

Pete let his breath out. "Is he—is he—?"

"Yep, he's dead as nails, sonny. That was a real

bullet. Never thought I'd have to kill one of Jim's animals." The vet shook his head ruefully.

Jupe tried to take his eyes off the spreading red stain. "Thanks, Dr Dawson," he said, swallowing hard. Then, "How did he get out?"

The vet shook his head. "It's my fault, I reckon. I needed to check him over, so I gave him a tranquillising shot. I stepped away for a few minutes while I was waiting for the drug to take effect. Next thing I knew he was on his feet and out of his cage. For some reason, the drug didn't work. I ran back to the jeep to get my gun—the one I use for killer hawks."

"Do you think somebody let the panther out?" asked Jupe.

"Who'd do a crazy fool thing like that?" countered the vet. "Anybody who tried that'd likely get mauled. No, I expect the cage door just wasn't locked properly."

"Might that drug you used have been tampered with? Weakened somehow by somebody?"

The vet looked shrewdly at Jupiter. "It could have happened that way, son. I leave my medical kit around a lot. Never saw no reason to distrust anybody here." He shook his head. "It sure beats me. Appears as if somebody sure has it in for Jim Hall. The shame of it is he's such a real nice fellow."

Pete leaned over the panther. "I guess you had to shoot to kill then, didn't you?"

"That's right, son. That baby might look like an overgrown pussy cat to you boys, but take it from me he was a real mean killer. If he'd got away, there's no telling what might have happened." He cocked his head and addressed the boys in a sharper tone. "What are you boys doing up this way, anyhow? Jim told me you'd be over at the movie set today watching George acting in the movie."

"We were there," Jupe started lamely, "but then —we thought we'd look around."

Dawson eyed Jupe and Bob and Pete in turn. "Jim told me you fellers were investigators." He smiled thinly. "Find out anything yet?"

Jupe shook his head. "No, sir. We're still confused."

"Can't say I blame you," the vet said. "Lots of confusing things happening round here lately. Things that don't make no sense at all. Want to hear one of the most confusing things about it?"

The boys looked at him questioningly.

Doc Dawson put a small cigar in his mouth, spat, put a match to it, inhaled smoke, and spat again. Then he levelled the thin cigar at them. "I'll tell you, then," he said. "Every time you kids show up here, another animal breaks loose. Think it over. Am I right?"

The boys looked at one another.

Dawson broke the spell by laughing sourly. "I'm right," he said.

He kicked at the body of the black panther. "I'll be right back for this baby," he said. "In the meantime, boys, I got some good advice for you—"

"What's that, sir?" asked Bob.

"Watch yourselves at all times," the vet said curtly.

He turned on his heels and walked away. In a moment he had disappeared into the tall, waving grass.

16

Iron Bars

As soon as Doc Dawson walked away from the dead panther, Jupiter led the other investigators down the hill to the fence by the salvage yard. The boys looked over at the huge spread of scrap iron, covering several acres. Workmen could be seen here and there.

"What are we doing here?" Pete asked.

"We're looking for the smuggled diamonds," Jupe replied. "And we're looking for George's old cage."

"You think those diamonds are still in George's cage?" asked Bob.

"I doubt it," said Jupe. "That cage has been around a long time. But we might get some ideas if we could find it."

"But, Jupe," complained Pete, "if the diamonds

aren't in the cage, what are they in? What do we look for? A little paper bag?"

Jupe scowled. "Frankly, Pete, I don't know what the diamonds would be in. I don't think Olsen or Dobbsie know either, or they would have found them by now."

"Olsen and Dobbsie looked all over this place last night and didn't find anything," said Bob. "What makes you think we'll have better luck?"

"It's daylight," said Jupe. "That should give us an advantage."

"Craziest thing I ever heard of," muttered Pete.

A workman who had been near the fence moved away, leaving the area clear. "Let's go," said Jupe.

The boys found the section of fence that had been pulled out of line the night before. It was an easy matter to loosen the metal upright again, and the wire netting with it. Seconds later, they had crawled into the middle of a junk pile that seemed to contain all the abandoned automobiles in the state.

Heavy clanking noises began on the other side of the salvage yard, punctuated by shrill whining sounds.

"Let's see how that metal shredder works," Jupe said.

He pointed to a huge crane. It was several hundred yards away, operating at the opposite end of the yard. As they watched, they saw a tiny figure in the cranehouse shift a gear. There was a complaining whine. A huge metal claw came up from behind a mound holding an old car.

The operator shifted a lever and the cranehouse swivelled to one side. Whining, the metal claw swung over the assorted debris of the yard. It stopped, causing the car to sway dangerously, and then lowered abruptly. The claw opened and the car dropped, landing with a heavy clank. Immediately there was a whup-whup-whup sound and the car jolted crazily forward.

"Conveyor belt," Pete said, standing on a pile of junk. "It's taking the car right into that shed."

The conveyor belt was a series of flat cars moving forward in steady jerks. When the old car disappeared into the mouth of the shed, the belt halted temporarily.

There was a shrill, screaming sound from the shed, a rising whine that blasted the air and threatened their eardrums with its intensity.

"Metal shredder at work," observed Jupe.

"Ugh!" said Pete. "It sounds as if the car is being eaten alive!"

The crane had swivelled again. Once more the huge claw rose in the air, swaying until it had seemingly found its prey. Then, with a whine, it pounced on another derelict car. Once more it fed the car into the shed.

Jupe turned away. "Okay. Now we know how it works. Let's get back to our own mystery."

The boys poked around for a while, without any luck.

"Maybe I'd do a better job if I knew what to look for," said Pete, kicking a piece of junk.

"Hold it, Pete," Jupe cried. "What's that?"

He ran over and picked it up carefully.

"It looks like a cage," Bob said. "Or maybe something that once was a cage."

"How can you call it a cage?" Pete demanded. "It doesn't have any bars. It looks like a broken old box."

"Perhaps the metal shredder has already processed it," said Jupe. "If you recall, the shredder selects metal from objects and discards the rest."

"Uh-Uh," Pete said as he dived off the pile. He came up grinning, holding a long, black iron bar. "That metal shredder is a fake," he said. "It can't tell iron from anything. What do you call this?"

Jupe was so pleased, he almost shouted with joy. "Good work, Pete! That might be what we're looking for. Let me see it, please."

Pete handed the bar over and Jupe promptly dropped it.

"Butterfingers!" Pete scoffed.

"No, I didn't expect—" Jupe bent to pick up the bar again. "That's odd," he said. "It feels heavy."

"Of course it's heavy," Pete said. "Why do you think I was complaining the other day when we had to unload a ton of these from your uncle's truck?"

Jupe stared down at the bar, his eyes gleaming thoughtfully. "I didn't notice. I'm certain the other one I had was—"

He stopped, his mouth open.

"What's wrong, Jupe?" asked Bob.

"N-nothing," Jupe said. He slung the bar across

his shoulder. "Quick! We've got to get back to our junkyard at once!"

"But why?" Pete protested. "If you're so happy with one iron bar, how do you know I can't find more?"

"Because," Jupiter stated as he moved away, "there aren't too many that bear the specifications I have in mind."

"Such as what?" Pete demanded.

"Such as containing smuggled diamonds," Jupiter answered, heading rapidly for the wire fence.

They didn't have too long to wait for Konrad to pick them up on his return trip from nearby Chatwick. On the ride home, Jupiter refused to be drawn into conversation. Instead, pinching his lower lip, he stared out of the window, nodding to himself several times as if to confirm certain inner convictions. Bob and Pete were accustomed to their leader's temporary fits of silence and knew he wouldn't explain himself until he was ready.

Once at the yard, Jupe hurried to his workshop. He stopped at the workbench—and cried out in dismay.

"It's gone!"

"What's gone?" asked Bob.

"The iron bar I picked up last night when Bo Jenkins chased us." He ran over to the junk pile hiding Headquarters and returned, looking puzzled. "The first bar I had has disappeared, too."

"What's this all about?" asked Pete.

Jupe shook his head impatiently. "I'll tell you later. Come on, I have to find Uncle Titus. Maybe he knows something."

Uncle Titus was across the street at the Jones' house, sitting and smoking his pipe. He nodded contentedly as the three boys approached.

"Howdy, boys," he said pleasantly. "Have a good time today?"

"Pretty good, Uncle Titus," Jupe began. "I wanted to ask—"

"We did pretty good here, too," interrupted his uncle. "Yes, sirree, had a good spell of business."

"What did you sell, Uncle Titus—some iron bars?"

His uncle rocked and nodded. "Right smart of you to guess, Jupe. Yes, sir, we did just that. Hans and your aunt scoured the yard for all we had. We needed them, you see," he added with a wink.

"What for, Mr Jones?" asked Bob.

"What for? To make cages, of course. Told you the other day we were going to, didn't I, Jupiter? Well, today Hans and me started to work on them, and then this feller comes in. His problem is he needs some big animal cages—and he needs 'em bad. Some kind of an emergency, I figure, where you suddenly need a lot of cages.

"Well, sir, I had to think fast. Y'see, we meant to fix 'em all up but we were still a few bars shy."

Jupe felt sick inside. "Was it that man who was here the other day? The one called Olsen?"

"Not that feller. Another chap. Very likeable sort of man. Truth is, Jupe, even though I had my

128

mind made up to save those cages for a circus, this chap's work was close enough to help me change my mind."

"It was?" Jupe repeated dully.

Titus Jones nodded, drew deeply on his pipe, and blew smoke. He finally went on. "Well, on account of him being such a nice chap and worried so, needing 'em so bad, I decided to co-operate. We all worked like the dickens fixing the cages and hunting for bars. Now your aunt saw you drop a bar near your workshop—that was the other day—and she picked that one up."

"Oh, Aunt Mathilda did?" Jupiter groaned.

His uncle nodded. "A good thing, too. We were still one bar too little even with that, until Hans found another one on your workbench, Jupe. We figured you had no earthly use for it. Bars and junk like that come in here all the time, you know, and you're always welcome to what you want—providing we don't need it for a customer. Right?"

Jupe nodded dumbly.

His uncle smacked the dottle from his pipe. "Well, that feller couldn't believe his eyes when we showed him we had the four cages all ready to go. Paid me a hundred dollars apiece, without my even painting 'em up. Said his animals would feel at home in 'em just like they were."

"You got those cages over in the Chatwick Valley, didn't you, Uncle Titus."

"Yep. At a big scrap yard. They didn't care about cages. Their main business was in junked cars. Had a teriffic machine to eat 'em up. Made a racket, it did."

Jupe gestured helplessly, his worst suspicions confirmed.

As Mr Jones stretched and stood up to leave, Jupiter had only one more question. "This man with the animals, Uncle Titus—the one you sold the cages to—did you get his name?"

His uncle smiled benevolently. "Of course I did. Easy one to remember, too." He squinted into the distance to remember the easy name. "It was, lemme see—yep, Hall. That was his name, all right. Jim Hall."

Jupiter stared at his friends.

17

Jupiter Explains

A CALL to the Rent-'n-Ride Auto Agency found Worthington available soon for another trip to Jungle Land. While waiting for him to arrive, the boys gobbled some lunch in Aunt Mathilda's kitchen.

"All right, Jupe," said Bob as the boys settled into the back seat of the Rolls-Royce. "It's about time you explained what's going on."

"It's very simple," said Jupe. "The diamonds are being smuggled by the Hall brothers in iron bars."

"Are you feeling all right, Jupe?" Pete asked. "That iron bar I picked up at the scrap yard and handed you—are you talking about that kind of bar?"

Jupe nodded.

"But that bar was solid iron," Pete said. "How can you smuggle diamonds in something like that?"

"You can't," Jupe said. "But you can smuggle diamonds in a hollow bar. Remember I told you that your iron bar felt different? Well, it was. It was a lot heavier than the one I picked up last night when Bo Jenkins was after us. And it was a lot heavier than the bar I put aside when we were unloading Uncle Titus's truck. It was so much heavier that suddenly everything clicked.

"I knew that I had hollow cage bars, and that Uncle Titus must have bought his bars and cages at the scrap yard where Jim Hall had tossed George's cage and probably others, too."

"But how did you know that the two bars you had contained diamonds?" asked Bob.

"Well, I didn't know for sure," said Jupe, "until I heard that Jim Hall had bought the cages from Uncle Titus. He never would have returned for them if the smuggled diamonds weren't still in them. It's just my bad luck that I had the bars and then lost them. I still don't know why he waited so long."

Pete looked puzzled. "I don't get it. If he knew

the diamonds were in the cages, why did he discard them in the first place?"

"Perhaps the heat was on," Jupe said. "He couldn't afford to have them traced to his property. My guess is he dumped them over the fence at the scrap yard as a temporary measure, thinking they'd be safe there and he could pick them apart later. But somehow they got mixed up with a lot of other junk there, and my Uncle Titus bought them from the yard owners, along with all the long bars and railings."

"That's possible," said Bob. "Mr Hall could have then asked the yard owners who bought the junk and traced it to your uncle's junkyard. Olsen and Dobbsie must have known about the bars, too. Now that I think of it, Olsen first asked for bars when he came to your uncle's yard. Remember?"

Jupe nodded.

"I wonder if one of those men was the mystery buyer," added Bob.

"Mystery buyer?" asked Pete.

"Yes, the customer who bought the pile of bars and railings from Mrs Jones when we were making our first visit to Jungle Land. Those bars might have had diamonds in them, too."

"Naw," said Pete. "Those bars were awfully heavy—don't forget I was the one who carried them. And they were much longer than all the cage bars we've ever seen."

"I'm inclined to agree with Pete," said Jupe. "I don't think it matters who bought those bars. It was probably an innocent customer. And, if it wasn't—well, Olsen and Jim Hall both showed up at our yard later, so they couldn't have found the diamonds earlier."

"Hey, Jupe," said Pete. "What about that bar you found last night? Where did that come from?"

"That one could have got loose and fallen out of a cage when Jim Hall was dumping it into the scrap yard. I wish I knew how many cages were involved here. We know what to look for now, but we don't know how much to look for."

"All those bars look alike," Bob put in. "How can anybody tell which is which? When the cages arrive, they're all in place. How would Jim Hall know which bars have the diamonds his brother Cal inserted?"

Jupe smiled mysteriously. "There's a way of knowing."

Bob and Pete looked at him sourly. They knew from past experience that Jupiter would never divulge the last remaining secret to a mystery until the last possible moment.

Bob frowned. "We still haven't solved the mystery we were called in to investigate," he said. "Who is making Jim Hall's lion nervous? And if Mr Hall is tied in with the diamond smuggling, who's letting his wild animals escape from their cages? He might lose Jungle Land if there's an accident."

"We'll know the answer to that when we put all the loose ends together," Jupe said. "It's possible Jim Hall himself let George out when we got there the first time, as a diversion. He might have let the gorilla loose, too, and pretended to go off looking for him. If you recall, he came right back to where the gorilla really was pretty fast."

"Bringing Doc Dawson and his stun gun and saving our lives!" Pete said. "I won't hold that against him."

"What about this morning?" Bob asked. "Jim Hall was on the movie set with George. He couldn't have slipped away to let the black panther out, could he? And have Doc Dawson cover up for him and say it was his own fault?"

"It's possible," Jupe said thoughtfully. "Doc Dawson might have an idea of what Jim Hall is up to. He might be trying to cover up for him and maybe to protect Mike, as well. Doc Dawson always seems to turn up when he's needed. That suggests to me that he is aware of the situation, and able to anticipate just what is going to happen next."

Soon the Rolls-Royce was entering Jungle Land.

"Drop us at the foot of the hill leading to the Halls' house, Worthington," ordered Jupe. "I think that we should arrive discreetly."

The boys walked up to the quiet white house on the hill. As they came close, they stopped to listen.

"Not a sound," Pete whispered. "Maybe he's already found the diamonds and cleared out."

Jupe pushed his lower lip out. "We'll have to go in, anyway. We owe it to Mike to explain."

Bob and Pete nodded agreement. Jupe took a step forward and stopped.

"What's wrong?" whispered Bob.

"I thought I heard something," Jupe said. "Maybe we'd better check the cage area before we go in."

He turned and the others followed him into the shadows of the clearing.

"Seems quiet," Jupe said. "I don't see—"

He was interrupted as something heavy was thrown over his head. Bob and Pete were caught the same way. The boys were grasped by strong hands. Their cries were muffled, and although they struggled and kicked, they could not get away from their surprise attackers. Helpless, they were carried along in total darkness.

18

Trapped!

COVERED by a heavy blanket, The Three Investigators were unable to make out the voices of their abductors. They were bouncing as if they were being carried over rough terrain. One of their carriers stumbled and complained loudly. Another voice curtly cut him off.

The caravan halted. Ropes were lashed round them. They felt themselves being lifted again and then heaved headlong on to a springy surface. A heavy door thunked shut.

"That oughta keep 'em out of the way," a voice said.

They heard receding footsteps and then silence. They struggled to straighten themselves, pausing as they heard another sound.

Whup-whup-whup---pp!

They felt themselves being jerked forward, then rocked back abruptly. There was a whining sound and a heavy crunch as if something had grabbed them from both sides. The whining sound became a groan. Suddenly they felt the odd sensation of being lifted.

"Goodness!" Bob exclaimed. "Are we riding in something?"

"Apparently," Jupe said. "And I don't like the sound of it. We'd better work fast. Try to slip the blanket off first. That way we won't suffocate, and we may be able to see where we are—and be heard!"

Following Jupe's directions, they pushed and pulled in turn. Gradually the heavy blanket over them was tugged down.

"Use your fingers," Jupe urged. "Keep pulling down and rolling the blanket under you."

They struggled to get free, their hearts thumping wildly as they heard the menacing sounds all around them. Something chattered and roared beneath them, and from above they heard groaning, creaking sounds that sent chills down their spines.

Suddenly they were rocking in a wide swinging arc.

"It's the claw!" Pete yelled.

In a last convulsive movement the boys jerked the blanket down from their heads.

They gasped.

Straight ahead they saw nothing but the sky.

Far below was the spread of junked cars in the scrap yard.

At either side were the huge metal talons of the giant claw, gripping the old car that they rode in. They were trapped in the air—and headed for the metal shredder! They began to yell for help, but the huge machine in the shed below started to chatter and scream, roaring out a series of deafening sounds.

Pete shook his head. "No chance! We can't compete with that monster. Not even if we yell our heads off!"

"Apparently the crane operator can't see us either," Jupe cried. "We've got to get out of these ropes so we can attract his attention!"

They struggled and rocked but the ropes held tight.

They heard a shrill whistle. Abruptly the giant claw dropped. Then, with a sickening lurch, they were falling to the ground.

They bounced as they hit. Almost immediately, they were jerked forward. They stopped, rocked, and were jerked forward again.

"We're on the conveyor belt now!" Jupe said. "We don't have much time. Come on—the metal shredding process takes place right ahead!"

Again they struggled, but it was to no avail.

Relentlessly the conveyor belt advanced.

They yelled again, but their voices sounded puny in the yard's roar. "Kick the doors!" Jupe yelled. "Maybe we can knock them open."

They tried to obey but their efforts were futile. The ropes lashed around them were too tight. Tied together as they were, they were unable to use their legs. They thrashed about uselessly, and fell back, exhausted.

"It's no use!" Pete gasped. "Our only hope is that somebody working the metal shredder inside sees us in time."

"I doubt that," Jupe said. "A processing machine like this is usually run by a computer. It's not a question of our not being metal. The car we're in *is!* The selective scanner couldn't possibly reject us until it was too late!"

"You're not kidding," a voice said.

They stared incredulously into the cold eyes of the hatchet-faced man!

"Get the door on the other side, Dobbsie," Hatchet-Face said.

Surprisingly, his touch was gentle, although they felt the strength in his hands as he lifted them out. As they rolled on the ground, the car they had been riding in jerked forward.

Staring wide-eyed, the saw it disappear into the shed, to be lost in a cloud of steam. Heavy clanking sounds reverberated and the machine inside screamed.

Jupe turned with a tremendous sigh of relief to

the two men. His expression changed suddenly.

Dobbsie was holding a long-bladed knife!

"Be reasonable!" Hatchet-Face said cajolingly. "We have to cut those ropes off you kids, don't we?"

Jupe nodded dumbly. He looked at Bob and Pete. They returned his mystified glance.

The beady-eyed man bent and slashed deftly with his knife. In a moment they were free.

As they rubbed their arms and legs to regain circulation, the hatchet-faced man looked down coldly at them. "Looks as if we got here just in time," he rasped. "What happened?"

"Somebody threw a blanket over us, tied us up, and threw us in a car," said Jupe. "I don't know if we were intended for the metal shredder, or not. We're grateful to you for preventing us having to find out."

"Any idea who did it?"

Jupe shook his head. "It happened too fast. We were rounding the corner of Jim Hall's house—" He stopped abruptly and glanced at the men. "How did you know we were trapped in the car?"

The hatchet-faced man sighed and looked over Jupe's head at the other man. "We happened to be in the yard. Dobbsie here thought he saw a moving kicking bundle being thrown into a car at the far end. That's a bit unusual, so we went to investigate. Whoever did it ran off before we could get over. Then the claw got you and dumped you on the conveyor track. We couldn't get the crane operator's attention or stop the belt moving. So we had to do it the hard way and drag you out ourselves."

Pete shivered. "I can't believe he would have done that to us. I just can't believe it!"

"Who, kid?" asked the hatchet-faced man. "And what do you kids know that's so dangerous somebody nearly had you killed because of it?"

Jupe lifted his head. "We're conducting an investigation," he said. "We have our suspicions but we're not at liberty yet to divulge any names."

The hatchet-faced man grinned. "Oh, you're not, eh? Maybe we should have kept out of it and let you continue your investigations—" he pointed to the throbbing shed " —in there!"

Jupe cocked his head. "As a matter of fact," he said, "both the actions of you and your friend have aroused our suspicions, too. But I don't suppose you have anything to do with the diamond smuggling, or else you wouldn't have rescued us."

Hatchet-Face looked at Dobbsie. "What'd I tell you? The kid is wise to the operation!" He looked down and laughed at Jupe. "I suppose you can tell us where they are, too."

"I suppose I can," Jupe said slowly. "But I won't."

Hatchet-Face jerked his head at the other man. "Come on, Dobbsie. We're wasting time. While we're here yakking, they could be getting away."

The beady-eyed man with the mashed nose came close to Jupe and raised a warning finger. "This is big time stuff, feller—not for kids. Watch yourselves!"

The menace in his powerful frame was unmistakable. He wheeled away to join his swift-moving companion, leaving The Three Investigators with a warning they could not afford to ignore!

19

In the Bag

YOUNG Mike Hall looked surprised when he threw the door open. "Jupe! Hi, fellows! C'mon in. We didn't expect you back today."

"I know," Jupe said as he entered the house. "Have Mr Olsen—the man you called Dunlop—and another man been here?"

Mike shook his head. "No, why?"

Jupe frowned. He wondered where they were. "I suppose your Uncle Jim is out, isn't he?"

Mike shook his head again. "What gave you that idea? He's in the back room with George, resting. Wait a second. I'll call him."

As he walked off, Jupe looked at Bob and Pete.

"It beats me, too," Pete said. "I was sure they were heading here."

"Maybe they're off looking for the cages," Bob said.

A cheery voice interrupted. "What cages?"

"Your old cages, Mr Hall," Jupe said.

Jim Hall looked surprised. "What are you driving at?"

"You ought to know, Mr Hall," Jupe said. "You're the one who bought back George's old cage, along with the other three, from my Uncle Titus."

Hall's face looked blank. "I—what?"

"You bought back the cages, and took them away," Bob put in. "The ones with the bars that hold the smuggled diamonds."

Jim Hall looked from one boy to the other with a dumbfounded expression. "Okay," he said. "Now you tell me. Maybe I'm not hearing so well today."

Pete shuffled his feet and look uncomfortable. "But I guess you didn't have anything to do with shanghaiing us and dropping us off at the metal shredder?"

Hall shook his head dumbly and turned to Mike. "What are your friends talking about?"

"I don't know," Mike said.

"You told us you had a problem," Bob said. "It was a mystery and you wanted our help. Who was making George nervous? Or what? But it turns out the mystery is how your brother Cal ships you diamonds from Africa, along with some animals. Some of the cage bars with the diamonds in them got lost somehow and that's why you had to buy the cages back from Jupe's Uncle Titus earlier today."

"You're crazy!" Mike burst in. "I've been with Jim every minute since early this morning. He hasn't stepped out of Jungle Land once today!"

Jupe looked up at Jim Hall. "You didn't?"

Hall shook his head.

"My Uncle Titus said he sold the cages to a man named Jim Hall. I'm sorry I didn't ask him to describe the man. I think I can guess now who it was—"

"Dobbsie?" asked Bob.

"It's possible," Jupe said. "Uncle Titus said it wasn't Olsen-Dunlop. It could have been Dobbsie." He looked up at Jim Hall again. "You don't know anything about any diamonds?"

"I don't even know what you're talking about," said Hall.

"Why did you get rid of George's cage?"

Hall shrugged. "It seemed wrong to keep him locked up in a cage when I was trying to train him with love and kindness. I felt we were losing touch every time I had to lock him inside again. Once Mike came to stay with us, I decided George had to be proven trustworthy. I got rid of the cage, had it thrown over the fence into the scrap yard, and that was the end of it. George became a regular member of the household, just like Mike and myself."

"But you kept the cage outside your house for a while after George moved in, didn't you?" Jupe persisted.

"Yes, until recently. I made up my mind to get rid of it completely when Jay Eastland came along and wanted to hire George for his movie. I didn't want him to get the idea George was still a wild animal. From that point on, Jay Eastland saw George only as a well-trained housepet."

Jupe looked rueful. "I owe you an apology, Mr Hall. It appears all my deductions and assumptions have proven false."

"We all make mistakes, Jupe. Maybe it's time you told me what this is all about."

Jupe explained from the beginning, starting with the arrival of the cages in The Jones Salvage Yard, and then the man named Olsen. "Mike says he works for Mr Eastland and is called Dunlop. But he told us his name was Olsen. A thin, hatchet-faced, light-haired man."

"I don't know him but I think I've seen him around the set," said Hall.

"He was looking over the scrap heap last night," Bob said. "Along with a man he called Dobbsie. They talked a lot about the smuggled diamonds. We couldn't figure out if they were part of a gang or what. They're the same two who rescued us a while ago when we were on our way into the metal shredder!"

Jim Hall listened carefully. When they had finished telling all they knew, he shook his head. "I'm sorry, boys, but I don't understand a single part of what you've said. Maybe it's true that these goings on made George upset and nervous. Maybe it's true that somehow diamonds are being smuggled in here. But I'll tell you one thing you can bet on," he added, his eyes flashing. "My brother Cal wouldn't have a thing to do with anything crooked!"

Jupe nodded and thought a minute. "Can you tell us what other cages you've discarded over the past few months?" he asked.

"We threw out two or three old cages a year ago," Jim Hall said. "But the only one lately was George's."

"Apparently that was the start of it, then," Jupe said thoughtfully. Abruptly he asked, "How is George feeling today?"

Jim Hall smiled. "First rate. He did a good job on the movie set this morning and he's been fine ever since. He's inside snoozing now. Doc Dawson was here and gave him a tranquilliser."

Jupe motioned to his companions. "Well, we'd better be going. We still have some work to do, fellows."

Mike Hall opened the door. "Come on back again when you can," he said. "I'm sure Jim doesn't blame you—"

"He should," Jupe said severely. "I had no business making an accusation before I had sufficient evidence. I owe you both an apology, Mike."

As Jupe went out, his foot caught on the threshold of the door and he stumbled across the porch. He grabbed for the porch post, yelled, and yanked his hand away.

"Oww!" he cried. He looked down at the drop of blood on his finger. "I just caught my finger on a splinter."

"Gosh, I'm sorry, Jupe," Mike said. "Come on inside. We'll find a Band-Aid for you."

"It's okay," Jupe said sheepishly as he went back in the door. He sucked his finger. "Just a little cut."

Mike snapped his fingers suddenly and pointed. "I was about to say it's too bad Doc Dawson isn't around to fix you up. Look—he forgot his medical kit."

Jupe looked at the worn, black leather bag sitting on a chair. "Would he mind if I helped myself to a bandage?"

"Are you kidding?" Mike said. "That's what it's for—emergencies. Help yourself."

Jupe opened the bag and reached inside for a roll of gauze wrapped neatly in blue paper. Holding it awkwardly, he fumbled with the protective cover. A small yellow piece of paper fluttered out.

Mike picked it up. "Looks like you dropped one of Doc's prescriptions, Jupe. Here, better put it back."

Jupe glanced at it automatically as it was handed to him. His lips moved wordlessly and he stared at it pop-eyed.

"What is it, Jupe?" asked Bob.

Jupe shook his head and looked at the scrap of paper again. "I can't believe it," he said slowly. Then he sighed a long sigh. "But, of course. Now the whole thing begins to make sense."

"What can't you believe?" asked Pete. "What makes sense?"

Jupe held out the scrap of torn paper. "Read it yourself."

They stared at the paper in Jupe's hand. It read:

DOX ROX NOX EX REX BOX

Mike looked mystified. "What does it mean?"

"It means a man we never suspected is behind it all," Jupe said. He shook his head ruefully. "It's all perfectly clear now."

"What are you trying to tell us now, Jupe?" asked Jim Hall.

"You won't like it," Jupe said. "It's Doc Dawson."

Jim Hall smiled thinly. "I don't think you know what you're talking about, son. Doc's an old friend. Let me see that piece of paper."

As he held out his hand, the front door opened.

A burly figure stood there. Head close-shaven, arm tattooed. "I came to pick up Doc's bag," he said. "He forgot it here."

His eyes narrowed as he saw the open medical bag, and then the small slip of yellow paper in Jupe's hand. His lips twisted angrily. "I'll take that, you snooping kid!" he roared.

Before Jupe could move, Bo Jenkins had snatched the paper from his hand. He crumpled it in his huge fist and reached for the leather bag.

Jim Hall spoke up mildly. "Hold it just a second, Bo. There's something going on here and—"

Jenkins made a sudden movement and pulled out a gun. "Stay out of it, Hall, if you know what's good for you. We got it all now and nothin's stopping us."

Jupe gulped. "You're the man who bought all the cages from my uncle—and gave Jim Hall's name!"

Jenkins grinned. "Wise apple, huh?"

Jim Hall whistled softly as the animal handler grabbed the black bag.

Heavy, padding steps sounded across the room. An ominous rumbling made Jenkins turn and stare. His jaw sagged and he paled.

A large, yellow-eyed lion stood there, head down and long tail twitching restlessly. The growling continued.

Instantly Jupe leaned against the door, closing it.

Jenkins whirled again at the sound, his gun jerking.

"Forget it, Jenkins," Jim Hall said calmly. "You're not going anyplace. One more step and George will have you for dinner." Hall turned to the lion. "Won't you, George?"

The lion slowly opened its cavernous mouth and moved forward.

There was a clattering sound as the gun fell from Bo Jenkins's fingers.

"That's better," Jim Hall said. He bent forward to retrieve the gun and waved the frightened man to a chair. The lion came forward and stopped at Bo's side, opening its mouth in a huge yawn.

"Now then, Bo," Jim Hall said pleasantly. "What can you tell us about some smuggled diamonds?"

20

End of the Puzzle

As they rounded a turn in the trail, Mike pointed ahead to a small house next to a barn. "That's Doc Dawson's place," he said. "The dispensary is in the back."

Sounds of hammering came from the barn.

Jupe smiled. "That's one thing he never figured on. When my Uncle Titus has something fixed, he does a very thorough job."

"What do you mean, Jupe?" asked Mike.

"You'll see in a minute," Jupe said mysteriously.

A small pickup truck stood in the driveway by the barn. Alongside it four cages lay tumbled on the ground. The grizzled vet stood next to one with a hammer raised in one hand. In the other he held a long pair of pliers.

He paused as Jim Hall strode up, flanked by the boys. His eyes flicked past them and narrowed.

"Howdy, Jim," he said. "Anything wrong?"

Jim Hall shook his head. He tossed the black leather bag at the vet's feet. "Heard you were looking for your bag, Doc. You left it at the house."

"Thanks, Jim," Dawson said. He gazed beyond them and frowned. "I sent Bo Jenkins—I thought—" He looked at the cages, scowling. "I need him to help—"

Hall nodded. "Bo's all tied up at the moment, Doc. Maybe we can give you a hand. What's the trouble?"

The vet looked at the hammer in his hand. "No trouble, Jim. Just wanted to make sure the bars are good and tight. Don't want any more accidents. That fellow Eastland will have every nickel of yours if one more animal gets away."

Hall smiled. "Thanks, Doc. I appreciate your concern." He looked at Jupe. "Can you tell which bars?"

"I think so, sir," Jupiter said. "But I'd need to borrow his hammer."

"No problem," Hall said. "Can you loan this young fellow your hammer for a moment, Doc?"

Dawson hesitated, then handed it to Jupe. "Guess so. What's up?"

"These young fellows are The Three Investigators. I hired them, you recall, to find out what's been making old George nervous. They've come up with some cock-eyed notion that it's all because of some smuggled diamonds."

Dawson grinned. "No kidding? Cock-eyed is right." He looked at Jupe. "Any idea where they might be?"

"Yes, sir," Jupe said. "If you would just step aside for a moment, please."

"Why, sure," Dawson said easily, moving away. "Only go easy with that hammer, son. I wouldn't want those bars loosened after all the trouble I've been to tightening them up."

"You didn't tighten them up," said Jupe. "Hans and Uncle Titus did, back at our junkyard."

Doc looked surprised.

"You'll notice," Jupe continued, "they didn't put back the bars the way they were. Uncle Titus is very fussy about giving a customer no reason for complaint. So he and Hans bolted and screwed the bars in this way so they wouldn't work loose as they did before."

"Very interesting," Dawson said.

"So you can't hammer them off," Jupe said. "All you can use the hammer for is this, really." He walked around the cage beating at the bars with the heavy hammer. He stopped at the fourth one from the end, then continued through the others, pausing once more. He returned to the fourth one again.

"There are two on this cage," he said.

Dawson glanced at Jim Hall. "Any idea what he's talking about?"

Hall frowned. "I'd rather wait and see, Doc."

"Most of these bars are rusted," Jupe said, "indicating they've been outside and exposed to the weather a long time. They could belong to any of the cages Mr Hall discarded. But this rusty one gives off a different sound—it's hollow, you see. So my deduction is this one could have come from George's cage.

"This one here," Jupe continued, striding to the opposite end of the cage, "is hollow, too." He struck it with his hammer. "It's still in good condition because it just came in recently. It's from the gorilla's cage. Bo Jenkins took it off the night the gorilla arrived. The gorilla twisted the other bars apart and broke out. I believe the gorilla went after Bo and he became frightened and ran, tossing the bar away in his panic. I happened to come across it by accident."

"But how did Bo Jenkins know you had it?" Mike asked.

"He was out looking for it later that night," Jupe said. "He heard us and pointed his torch at us and saw me holding it. He'd seen us before and probably Doc Dawson told him who we were and where we came from. He came to the yard and found my uncle working on the cages. He must have been delighted when he heard they'd have to search the yard for extra bars. He couldn't be sure, but there was a good chance the gorilla bar would turn up. Of course, he had no idea that George's bar was around, too."

"How can you be sure you've found the right bars here?" asked Mike.

"I can't, until we take the bars off," said Jupe. "But I expect we'll find the diamonds in them, since I used the smugglers' own method of locating them."

"How do you know that?" asked Mike.

"The cable told me, and Doc Dawson confirmed it. The cable said, 'DOX ROX NOX EX REX BOX.' Which means, knock on the bars of the lion's cage and you'll find the diamonds inserted at the docks. EX, I would guess, stands for 'out

152

of'—take the lion out first. A wise precaution, considering what happened with the gorilla.

"Now, do you recall what Doc did last night when the gorilla was brought back? Doc tested all the bars on its cage with the hammer. He did the same thing with the panther cage. At the time it merely seemed an odd way to test the strength of bars. But Doc was actually testing for diamonds— probably trying to make sure Jenkins had picked the right bar, or possibly making sure there were no others. Once they had the manner of smuggling arranged and the cable informing them how to look for the hollow bars—it was easy. Any bar that sounded hollow would contain diamonds."

Jupiter turned to Doc Dawson. "May I have the pliers, please?" Doc silently handed them over.

Jupe clamped the long pliers to the top bolt on the rusty bar he'd singled out. A few hard turns and the bolt came off. Jupe stooped and repeated the action with the bottom bolt. He took the hammer and knocked the bar through the drilled slots in the boards. As it came out, Hall and the boys crowded around.

Jupe knocked the top cap off the bar, then turned it over and struck it with the hammer. A thin trickle of greasy yellow stones came out.

"Those are diamonds?" Pete asked.

Jupe nodded. "Rough, uncut diamonds, Pete. They look like ordinary rocks and pebbles when they're found."

"Gosh!" exclaimed Bob. "There's a ton of them there."

Jupe smiled, looking down at the pile of dull stones. "Well, not a ton exactly, Records. Mr Olsen-Dunlop mentioned six hundred K's. He was talking about carats, I believe. A carat is worth approximately one thousand dollars. Allowing for some loss in cutting, we have a good half-million here. And with those in the gorilla bar, perhaps a million dollars' worth of diamonds altogether."

Jim Hall stared at the pile of stones and shook his head. "I'm sorry, Doc," he said. "I'm afraid you have some explaining to do."

There was no answer.

Jim Hall looked up, and twisted his head in surprise. Dawson was gone. They heard the sound of the truck engine starting up.

"He's getting away!" cried Pete.

The truck backed off with a roar as the boys started for it. Almost immediately two cars came from the trees and braked to a quick stop behind it, blocking the driveway. Two men leaped out.

"Hatchet-Face and Dobbsie!" cried Bob.

They grabbed Dawson as he jumped from the cab, and brought him forward to the barn.

"What's going on? Who are you two?" demanded Jim Hall.

Jupe pointed. "That one's Mr Olsen—he's been after the bars from the beginning."

"No," said Mike. "His name is Dunlop. He works for Jay Eastland."

The hatchet-faced man shook his head. "Sorry, boys—but you're both wrong. Stevenson's the name."

He flipped open his wallet and held it out.

Jupe's face reddened. "His card says Stevenson, all right." He looked up at the grinning man. "We thought you were part of the gang."

"Customs agents have to act mysterious, son," the man explained. "Dobbs here is with the Treasury Department. We're both working for the same firm—the United States Government. And we've been trying to break up this smuggling ring for a long time."

Dobbs gestured to the pile of stones lying on the ground. "Looks like the kid saved us a lot of trouble. We knew Dawson was getting diamonds, but we couldn't move in until they actually showed up. We didn't know exactly where they were and that's the kind of evidence that's needed."

"You'll find some more in another bar," Jupe said.

The Treasury agent kicked at the pile of stones. "Now all we have to do is find the other man—Bo Jenkins. He seems to have disappeared."

"You'll find him back at my house," said Jim Hall. "He'll be waiting for us."

The two men looked startled.

"He's not going anywhere," Jim Hall stated. "George is looking after him."

Dobbs looked at him wide-eyed. "George—the lion?"

Jim Hall nodded.

Stevenson grinned. He clapped Jupe on the shoulder. "Okay, Investigator—you already found half a million. Would you like to try for another?"

Jupe stepped forward to the cage. Pointing to the second bar he had selected, he said dramatically, "You will note, gentlemen, that this bar is not as rusted as the first one that was extracted from the lion's cage. The gorilla was a recent arrival and therefore—"

Bob and Pete exchanged grins. They knew how their leader loved to make the most out of a situation.

Doc Dawson laughed harshly. His shoulders sagged. He looked like a man who had bet a lot of money and lost.

"Hurry it up," he said. "I'd like to see how much I lost before I tell you everything."

21

Some Questions from Mr Hitchcock

A WEEK later, The Three Investigators sat in Mr Hitchcock's office, being congratulated.

"Thank you, sir!" chorused the boys.

"There are a few small points I should like to have cleared up," Mr Hitchcock told them. "This barbarous device—the metal shredder—am I to assume that your nearly fatal engagement with it was accidental?"

"Yes, sir," Bob said. "Bo Jenkins and Doc

Dawson tied us up and tossed us into an old junked car. They did it merely to get us out of the way. They never expected that the crane would drop the car on the conveyor belt."

Alfred Hitchcock nodded. "I would hope they would be more careful next time, if indeed there should ever be one, about the process they select for discouraging interlopers." He laced his fingers together. "This Hank Morton person—where does he fit in? Did he let George out deliberately and then wound him? And why was he running away the night the gorilla escaped? Was he involved in that, too?"

"No, sir," Bob said. "No to all of those questions. He came back to Jungle Land after being fired because he was suspicious of Doc Dawson. According to Hank Morton, Dawson made it look as if he had mistreated the animals, and Jim Hall took his word for everything. Dawson, of course, was trying to replace him with Bo Jenkins. When Morton came back, Doc decided to fix him for good. He let George out himself, planning to blame it on Morton.

"George cut himself accidentally out in the jungle. I guess he didn't know how to take care of himself out there, since he grew up in captivity. When Morton led us out to him, he was only teasing us. He knew George and could handle him. But when he stepped away for a minute, Bo Jenkins found him and hit him over the head. So Morton was blamed for that, too.

"That night when the gorilla broke loose,

Morton was trying to find Bo Jenkins. Instead he ran into the gorilla and was frightened away, just as Bo Jenkins was."

"What about the panther's escape?" asked Mr Hitchcock. "Did Doc Dawson engineer that?"

"No, sir," replied Pete. "At least, he said he didn't. We think it was a real accident. We're just grateful that Doc saved our lives. Mr Stevenson said that might be a point in Doc's favour when his case comes to trial."

Alfred Hitchcock glanced down at the papers on which Bob had summarised the adventure. "Ah, yes, Mr Stevenson, the government agent, also known as Olsen and Dunlop. You say he was planted with the Jay Eastland movie company by the authorities, to watch the smugglers?"

"Yes, sir," Jupe said. "He happens to be an expert on firearms and was available to Jay Eastland in that capacity. Eastland was acting so violently against Jim Hall, however, that he aroused Stevenson's suspicions. As it turned out, Eastland had nothing to do with the smuggling itself. But he was trying to take advantage of the contract Jim Hall had agreed to. He could have used an extra fifty thousand dollars and was hoping to pin something on Hall. But he couldn't, and since filming is over, Jungle Land is safe."

"Now as to the smuggling itself," said Mr Hitchcock. "Doc Dawson enlisted the aid of this Bo Jenkins to help retrieve the hollow bars. The diamond shipments originated in Africa, taking advantage of Cal Hall's deliveries of animals to his brother here. Was Dawson the ringleader? Did he plan the entire operation or was he merely an accessory? Exactly how did he fit in?"

"Doc Dawson planned it all," answered Jupe. "The diamonds were stolen from the surface portion of a deposit at Mwadui in the Shinyanga district of Tanzania. The smugglers followed Cal Hall to the port of Dar es Salaam and there switched the cage bars, first on George's cage, then on the gorilla's. When George left Africa, they alerted Doc Dawson with that coded cable."

"And why didn't Doc Dawson take the diamonds from the lion's cage as soon as it arrived?" Mr Hitchcock asked Jupe.

"Because he was expecting a gorilla to arrive with more diamonds soon afterwards. Only two shipments were planned. I guess he figured that the first lot were safe where they were, hidden in the cage bar, so he could wait till the second lot came and then clear out with a million dollars' worth of gems. But the gorilla didn't come for a long time. Meanwhile, Doc Dawson came down with the flu. While he was sick, Jim Hall threw out the lion's cage. It got broken up in the scrap yard and the bars misplaced. By the time Doc caught up with it, it was too late.

"It was also too late because by then the authorities were on to the smuggling operation. Stevenson wouldn't tell us how they learned about it—said he was sorry but he couldn't divulge his sources. When he and Dobbs got Dawson with the evidence, his confederates in Africa were rounded up."

The director tapped Bob's report again. "You surmised that George was being made nervous by the various attempts to get at the bar with the diamonds. Were you correct in that assumption?"

"Yes, sir. At first, I think, George was only restless because he was cooped up in the house at night. But then Stevenson and Dobbs started prowling around, which upset George."

"I still do not understand," rumbled Alfred Hitchcock, "why Doc Dawson, a respectable veterinarian, would become a diamond smuggler."

"That's easy," offered Pete. "He was a smuggler *before* he came to Jungle Land. He'd been through Africa and pulled various small jobs there years before. When he found out about Cal and Jim Hall's operation, it seemed perfect for his plans. So he joined up with them, using his skill with animals to get by, while he planned the entire diamond operation in Tanzania. He really did love animals, but he also loved the excitement of getting rich quick and dangerously."

"Not to mention criminally," added Mr Hitchcock. "I believe we are well rid of the fellow. He failed in his biggest attempt, the always tempting million-dollar haul. And you boys thwarted him by dint of clever deductions and perseverance. I'm proud of you all. You solved a most perplexing mystery."

"Mystery is our business!" said Jupiter Jones.